A PLACE

BURY HORSES

For my father, and all others,

Fighting silent wars.

PART ONE:

"OUR BROTHERS EARNED MEDALS UPON DISTANT SHORES."

PINE OAKS, OREGON
In the night, at around 3:00AM

I have this dream, every now and again. It's this cruel thing; woke up from it just now. It's stormy outside. It's late, too. I can't think, so I stand up. The bed is slick with sweat – damp mildew, my body's way of showing discomfort. I have this dream. I had it tonight.

It starts the same – *I'm with Alice, in the park. The one near where we lived in Portland, before the split. Before Wyatt. I'm running my hands through her hair – sandy blonde streaks of sunlight that frame a sun-kissed face. Her eyes are the color of an evergreen's leaves in autumn. I can't forget that color; can't. We're sat on a blanket, on a slight hill – lights and distant sounds of laughter fill the air in a cacophony. It's loud, but I hear her above all of that.*

'Joel, hey,' she says, and I nod. I hang on every word. I had dozed off, running my hands through the silky blonde shimmer of sunlight that is her hair. She's silhouetted by a slowly setting sun; the sky the color of napalm, of something beautifully deadly – the sun sets, and the sky is lit aflame. She's a shadow, carved in front of me – a beautiful darkness born from the dying of the light. We've

~ 1 ~

been there for hours, though I don't remember what we did during any of it. I know it's a dream, because we're happy. I speak softly to her, and I hear the whistle of the wind through the branches of the tree we sit under. I smell a barbeque that is being packed up by a family at the foot of the hill.

'I'm here,' I say. She laughs, places her hand on the one that I've rested on her face.

'I know,' she says. I smile. We kiss. A passionate thing. She pulls away first, and her smile melts any ice in my soul. 'I'm glad you came to see me,' she says. I nod.

'I'm not going, you know, anywhere. Not for a while yet.' I already feel like I have, however. Like I'd left a piece of myself somewhere oceans away.

She pours a glass of wine from the bottle I don't notice we had ~~have~~. *Two glasses of dark red are filled, and one is passed to me. We gently tap the glasses together; the clink soft and gentle, barely audible.*

'Cheers, baby,' she says. We drink. She leans in for another kiss, and I wake up.

I have this dream most nights. It has been years, now – time, it seemed, couldn't forget Alice either. I've had it again tonight, and I can't sleep. Nothing on TV. Never is at this time.

A PLACE TO BURY HORSES

I stare out of the apartment window; a single thing which lets a little of the world into mine. I see the main road of Pine Oaks; the street quiet in the night. A gentle neon sign pings at me from across the street, whorish and red. Chinese food. I cross my arms by the window; and simply stare out for a moment. I see a pair of men, leaving a bar. One of them is shouting, loudly, whilst his other friend is putting all his effort in staying upright. I can't hear what they say. One of them is getting married. Probably the guy who's forgetting how to use his legs.

I go over to my kitchen; a thing that's a messy construct of white chipped wood, and cold hard steel. I make coffee. I never drink it, save for when I can't sleep. Keep the dreams away, till the dawn.

I go back to the TV again, going through static and images of people; my mind so strung out with sleepiness it makes no sense. I flick through two more channels of pure, brilliant electric snow and stand up, turning the TV off for the final time tonight. Fuck it. There is never anything on anyway. I take my place by the window again, checking the clock hung by the TV. 4:00AM, now. The sky is taking the color of a healing bruise. I cough a few times, and it's making my head spin. In the distance I see thunder hammer away at the world, a screaming crescendo of blue flame that licked down from the sky. I watch it fork over a mountain, fade away. There's little in the way of rain. I nod at nothing.

A PLACE TO BURY HORSES

I see a car pull up at curb below. It's a beautiful, expensive car – not the kind you see around here anymore. I see a woman get out, wearing gym gear. She's wearing sunglasses, and I don't see the driver or the other passenger, as the windows are tinted and the angle is all wrong. She's got hair the color of midnight, tied up loosely. The red neon sign across the street highlights the sheen of sweat which is dancing across her face. I see her stand out, reach for a gym bag in the car. She's turning to the apartment door – the main one, but then stops. I can't hear, but she's speaking to someone in the car. She turns, once away, and then back. She sighs, and runs a hand through her black hair. She gets back in the car, and stays in it for another ten, fifteen minutes. I finish my coffee, and place the cup on the windowsill. The woman gets out of the expensive car again, and I see she's paler, now – her clothes are stained with sweat, and she spits a few times onto the curb. She has an envelope in her hands, and she closes the car door so loud I can hear it from the closed window, through the chipped and cobweb strewn glass. The girl watches the car speed away, before turning. She runs a hand through her hair, before putting a hand to her face. She wipes the sweat from her face, or maybe she wipes away tears, and glances, casually, up at me. We look at each other for a moment, before I turn away. I hear thunder boom in the distance, a war drum from some higher form of being than me.

I had this dream tonight, which woke me up. I have it all the time.

A PLACE TO BURY HORSES

*

In the morning, I wake up with a pain behind my eyes.
Feels like someone cut my skull open, left burning coals behind
them. It's the lack of sleep, and the amount of stress. I look at my
radio clock, by the bed. 7:00AM. I cough, and the room spins.
Christ. I stare up at the slowly rotating ceiling, notice the crack in it.
I wonder about the girl who I saw last night. Didn't recognize her.
New? Maybe. I don't know my neighbours, mostly because I never
want to meet someone else who ended up in this place. Three people
were shot to death here, last year. The walls are threatening to topple
– a tenement disaster waiting to happen. I wonder what would
happen if the whole place caught flame. An errant spark in a gas
main. The whole building a roman candle, a totem lit to show how
America works now. We skip out on the things we need, such as
safety, security, for the thing we want – money.

I stand up; numb tired legs. I stretch, heading out of my
bedroom into the bathroom. I piss, the porcelain seat an off white
color due to age. I yawn, brush my teeth. Get showered. Can't think
straight. Too tired.

I head out into the living room, looking at the dusty computer
in the corner. I put the TV on, KATU. Oregon News. A man in a
blue suit and a black tie, his hair trendy and short, looks into the
camera behind a desk.

'Good morning Oregon! I'm your host Greg Slaugh, and we've got some really great stuff coming up during the breakfast hour...'

He barely gets through the word "hour" before I turn it off. The guy looks like one of the puppets from *Thunderbirds*. I can't deal with that. Fake people. Fake world.

I head to the front door, and move to the corridor. Check the mail. Wyatt's birthday today. Nine years old. A lifetime and a child ago, I was a different man.

I head down stairs, where I bump into a man with skin the color of chalk. He twitches and shivers. I know him as Jay. I don't know the rest of his name. Frankly, I only knew the letter his name began with. Tweaker. Could see the way that life had treated him by taking a second to look him in the eyes.

'Yo, Joel!'

'Hi, Jay.'

'Good, ah, day, huh?'

'Yeah.' Jay looks past me. I nod. 'I need to check the mail. Have a good day, yeah, Jay?'

'Sure, my man. My bro. Ha. Yeah man.'

I know what's wrong with Jay. He has methamphetamine flashbacks, sees things that aren't there. I never ask what he sees, but judging by the way his eyes focus sharply, I'm guessing something bad. I wonder if he sees himself as a child, young, free. I wonder if it scares him, seeing what he was and could've been. It does me.

I stand in front of my mail box. I have a TV Guide, a takeout menu. I'm looking at the menu when I feel someone stand next to me. It's the girl from last night. She was new. Just moved it. Her hand reaches for the mail slot next to mine, and I see flowers tattooed there. Roses, with dangerous thorns. It's cut off by the grey Nike hoody she's wearing, but judging by the way it looks; her whole arm is covered in them, though I can't be sure. I can't help but look. The girl is wearing sunglasses again, and I realize she is looking at me a few seconds after I gaze at her arm. She smiles, and her voice is quiet, yet eloquent. It reminded me of confidence, purely distilled.

'So, uh, hey.'

'Hey,' I say, turning away. I look into the mail slot, and see no more parcels, no more cargo. The girl is young; I see that as I'm closer now. I lock my mail box, and nod at her politely. I'm walking away when I hear her call back to me. I reach the foot of the stairs, and place my hand on the metal railing.

'I'm uh, I'm new here. Name's Christy.'

'Joel,' I say, not turning. I head upstairs. There was too much heart in that girl, I could see. It wouldn't last. Life hadn't left you too much to live with, if you ended up here.

~ 7 ~

*

I stare at the computer; a blank page glows at me. I have work at 6:00PM. I have the time to do what I need to do. I just can't think, or focus. I think it's because of that dream, or maybe the lack of sleep. My brain isn't firing on all cylinders. It feels rotten, slow. Decayed, like bones in a desert. My mind was dry.

'Fuck,' I say, standing up. I go to the coffee machine, make another. It's shitty, but it's mine. I have no qualms about it – you make do with what you have and be proud of it. I walk past my cell phone, on charge by the microwave that I use too often.

I used to be terrified of the phone, people calling. Alice used to call, and it'd gnaw a hole in my chest that was biting blackness. It was after Wyatt. Eventually, I changed numbers. I threw my phone off the pier. Didn't care anymore. The day was some bleak thing that was a differently colored night – and Alice was gone. Wyatt was gone. We were gone. I stand by the window, seeing the people as they enter stores and come out with bags. I watch a young couple holding hands, and they both have face paint on. They look like tigers.

Young love is like that, I think as I turn away – ferocious, hungry. It is strangely apt, though I doubt they get the symbolism quite like me.

I sit back by the computer, cracking my knuckles. I don't know what the story brings, only that I have to write it. Get something accomplished. Get it right. Prove I can to myself, if no one else.

I rest my hands on the keys and begin to compose. I write about two teenagers, who do one bad, stupid thing – and the dark of the world swallows them whole.

*

PINE OAKS, OREGON
10.00AM

It wasn't a lot, but it was enough. A few pages of something that didn't exist before. I light a cigarette, looking at the screen, scrolling. It's rough, janky – but still, it didn't exist before. I lean back on my chair, and smile. I hear a few of the folks upstairs. They're arguing again. I don't know their names, but I think the husband is called Paul. His wife I don't know the name of, but I've seen her before. I helped her with her grocery shopping, once. When I first came here. So long ago. I stand up, and stretch again. I'd go for a run, but I haven't in years. I'd probably throw something out. I think about maybe going to a bar, and decide to. I could sober up by the time I had work.

I grab a jacket and head out. I pass Christy, carrying cardboard boxes through the open door. She's struggling to get a handle on one of them. I hear the clinking of glass from inside. Precious cargo, travelling so far. I stop when she sees me leave.

'Oh, uh, hey. Joel, right?'

'Yeah. I, ah, shit, let me help.' I step forward, and she shakes her head.

'It's cool,' she says. She nearly trips, but she puts the box down in the doorway to the apartment easily enough. She stands back up, a little breathless. We live on the third floor, and who knows how long she's been doing this already. Not my business. I smile at her. She smiles back, friendly. I smell something like strawberries as I walk past.

'Hey, I kinda need to do some grocery, you know, shopping later,' she says. I turn. 'You could show me around, you know. I haven't got a clue what's around here.'

'Sure. Not much to be found. But sure.'

'Where you going now?'

I'm halfway down the stairs when I speak.

'Drinking.'

*

Pine Oaks is a small town to the south-east of Portland if you go inland. It gets a bad rep, sometimes; like all small towns that claim to be cities. It's a little rough around the edges, but it works. There's something raw in it that I can't put my finger on, as I'm walking through the streets to this little bar I know. It's hidden away – down the wrong alley. They open early, and it's built for the disquieted souls who need the booze to stay afloat. We've had a few celebrities – we had the writer Robert Hull come through. He used to come to the library I work at, before he up and vanished. It also has a little bit of history that it's ashamed of – last year, in my apartment building, three people were murdered. It was tied to some big murder spree at a town up the road a ways, Point Truth. I've never been, never plan to. The place is haunted by ghosts, I'm sure.

People tend to wash up adrift here from Portland. That's a fact born of figures. It's irrefutable. Sometimes people lived here, chose to – more than that, they didn't. It was a stop gap, with just enough charm of every kind that it could sink its teeth into you.

The bar is called *Robins*, and styles itself after an Irish pub. It's alright. I'm the only one in at this time. I usually always am. Sarah, the owner and bartender, stands behind the counter to the left, arms folded. She's resting with her back against the bar, looking up at a TV. Liquors stand against a reflective mirror, and stools all stand up along the counter. To the right are a couple leather booths, and a small area with a round table and a few chairs around it. Bathrooms next, then nothing. Sarah doesn't turn, but does speak.

'Hey, Joel.'

'Sarah.'

'You wanting hun?'

'Usual.'

A PLACE TO BURY HORSES

A finger of whisky, Ruger Rose, is put in front of me. Sarah is a little younger than me. She knows how the world works though. A single mother.

'You okay?'

'Yeah.' I sip the whisky, the taste strong and not too pleasant. I don't drink because I like it. I drink because there's nothing else for me. I nod at the TV, and Sarah pours herself a glass, too.

'What's going on?'

'Oh, some shit about illegal raves at Crooks Hollow. That place, damn. It's just parties all the time.'

'It has to be somewhere.'

'Some new drug, or something. Kids are all over using it. *White Claudia.*'

'Nice name,' I say, finishing my whisky. I order another finger. Sarah gives me it. A few hours whittle away, the minutes and seconds incalculable. I lose them in the bottle. They spill over, and I can't catch them again. I reach for them, but I can't. They're lost.

*

I get to work for about Five Forty Five. I work at the library as a security guard. An old building, filled with new things. A symbol of this – once, a row of books were thrown away to make space for a computer desk. We were replacing things. The world works that way.

The new IT lab had been broken into a couple times, things taken that were too expensive to replace indefinitely and repeatedly. I don't mind it – it's easy work, and the whole time I've worked here, there hadn't been a problem. I see Liv at the main central reception of the Library and I wave. She's a quiet soul. She has a scar on her shoulder I saw once, at a Christmas party I came to for five minutes before leaving. I never ask, though I know the shape of it – a knife. A thin sliver of white that stares out of the dark caramel of her skin. She speaks quietly. I think she's spent a long time somewhere dark, and she couldn't quite climb all the way out of it. She tried, but left a piece of herself there.

'Hey Joel,' she says, and I smile and return the greeting. She smiles once, sheepishly, before lowering her gaze back to the Mac in front of her. Her fingers dance along the keys and I see her leave me for her work. I start my rounds, but still feel booze in me. I look out of the window for a moment, as the sun sets over Pine Oaks. The town hall stands like a monolith drenched in the setting day. I smile at the beauty of it before turning back to rows of books. I sit down and read one, but I can't remember the title, or author. Don't think to look. I think it's by Olivia Amber, but I can't tell. Can't remember. Been drunk since.

A PLACE TO BURY HORSES

I see a young man in the IT Lab, writing feverishly on the keys. He's copying notes from an old book or some journal. White T shirt, blue jeans, dark shoes. His hair is brown and semi long, pushed back from his face. There's softness to him, and a beard frames his mouth. I nod, and he raises a hand almost in salute. I don't know him, but feel like I do, and I see him leave later. I check the IT Lab, and all is there. I see a young woman a little later – nine forty five, near enough fifteen minutes before close. She's young, pale. She's sat crossed legged in an aisle, and I see she might be homeless. She sees me, before looking away nervously. I speak to her quietly, not too close.

'Hey,' I say, 'library closes in fifteen. You got somewhere to go?'

'I...yeah. I, I... I lost track.'

I run a hand down my face. Hangover is kicking in. Head's pounding like a war drum, softly and distant but there. I look over to Liv, now sat idly, staring at the screen while chewing a pencil. I speak to the girl, who's already standing up.

'Ten PM sharp, go to the front desk. Liv'll call you a cab. I'll give her money to get you where you need to. Places aren't safe this time of night.'

The girl looks at me with eyes that shine like I'd given her the world. She smiles, the cute shy way that belie broken hearts.

'I...thank you.'

'No worries,' I say, and continue. I leave twenty dollars with Liv, tell her the score. She nods, smiling. I nearly ask her for a drink, but don't.

Always nearly, never doing.

*

I leave work, shower. I go to type away at the book again – but don't. Time for that tomorrow. I have a whole night ahead of me. May as well let the world spin that little bit more. I hear laughter on Main Street, and the beginnings of thunder over head. I don't acknowledge either fully. I get dressed, head out into the night.

I pass a group of young women, holding hands and their heels clattering. One of them whistles at me, and I ignore them. They all laugh, drunkenly, before telling me to fuck off. I smile to myself, and then head into *Robin's*. The bar's full, and I smoke a cigarette outside whilst music and laughter leaks out into the night. A woman comes up to me; her face painted and heavily made up. A few drops of rain begin to fall. She looks up, raises a hand. Her eyes are sunken into the dark hollows of her eye sockets.

'Aw shit,' she says. She catches me looking at her, my cigarette a candle in the dark. Like a lighthouse on a distant shore. 'You got a spare?'

'I do.' I give her one, light it for her too. She breathes heavily. I see her teeth, jagged broken dark things. Junkie. I notice, too, the way she's looking at me.

'You, uh, you got any money? I just, you know. A little?'

'Yeah.'

'I could, uh...you know, I...if you, you had some money, I could...you know...'

'You're bad at hooking,' I say. I stamp my cigarette out on the curb. 'Stop.'

I don't know why I act how I do. Wonder if anyone does – how the little things build, till kindness burns to regret then anger. I wonder.

I leave her there in the rain, and head inside. The bar is full – too full. I'll stay for one, then go back home. Music is playing, loudly – some bluesy number that's fierce. I sit by the bar, on a stool. Sarah smiles at me, and places a glass of Ruger in front of me. I smile, raising the glass but then stopping. Noise all around. Can't think. I tap on the bar, a quick three raps of my knuckles. Sarah comes back.

'Sup, hun?'

'Make it a double.'

'Sure,' she says, smiling. She winks at me as she turns, and downs the whisky she'd put out for me. She comes back with a double, and I say to get one for herself. I sip the whisky, and I lose half of it by the time I realize someone is saying my name to my right. I lose track of time. I think of the way Alice used to smile at me over dinner. Christy is there, a black svelte dress on. I see now that the tattoo goes all the way up her arm – black flowers. Next to her is a Latino looking girl. Her hair is short, and brown. Trendy, though I'm not all the way sure. Christy is the one saying my name.

'Hey, Joel? Hello?'

'Ah, Christy, hey. I - sorry. Miles away.'

'Didn't take you for a...night out kind of guy, ahah.'

'I'm not.'

'Oh, uh,' she gestures to me whilst turning to her friend, 'this is my neighbour; Joel. Joel, Olive.'

Olive sticks her hand out, and speaks with slurred words. 'Like the gross things on pizza.' She laughs, and so does Christy. Christy's the more sober of the two, but she's slipping. I smile politely, and drink a little more deeply. I want out of there. Olive notices the tattoo on my wrist of a serpent.

'Hey, cool tat,' she says. Christy looks at it, and reflexively touches her own. Olive speaks again, taking my arm gently and rolling my sleeve up. She looks at it with a wry smile.

A PLACE TO BURY HORSES

'Where'd you get that?'

I speak gently, trying to get it under the music. 'Military.'

'Oh, woah,' says Olive. She touches the tattoo, and I squirm on the inside. She lets go after a second, and I drink more of my whisky. Christy moves her black hair behind her ear, and I see a little drunken gleam in her eye.

'Didn't know you were a soldier,' she says.

'I'm not,' I say. I finish my whisky, and stand up to leave. 'Not for a long time.' I leave the two, though I feel Christy keep her gaze on me for a moment. She calls 'Well, bye,' to me, and I call bye back. I can't tell if she heard me.

I make it home, seeing the woman from outside, who took the cigarette in the rain. She asks me the same question again, forgotten me already. Money for love. I decline, again. She calls me a faggot. I ignore her.

I'm sat in my living room, shirt off. Too warm. I'm drinking more. Things fade, bleed together. Memory goes. I dream again.

*

In my dream in a clearing of a darkened forest, I see a white horse by a stream. *A young woman leads me through the trees. Takes me a while to realize it's Christy. The horse drinks water deeply, eyes black stones against the snow of its color. Christy* *gently places a hand on its flank, and the horse doesn't react. She takes my hand gently, the roses and flowers on her pale skin visible. Her fingers entwine with mine for a moment, and she places my hand on the horse too. I feel the warmth of it, a heartbeat. Christy is smiling at me.*

The horse goes away. So does Christy. Fade away like time in the desert.

Now I'm stood in the police room in Portland, whilst Detective Ellis tells me how sorry she is, that he's been caught from his license plate. I'm in the old house in Portland, and Alice is crying. Halloween decorations are still up in mid-November. She's sat on the couch, her head in her hands.

I'm in Afghanistan, 2003. I'm watching an oil well burn, flames licking the night sky. I have the M16 in my hands, and I'm looking at the burning sky. Cold black death, illuminated by the fires of things older than me, finally dying in the cool plains of Afghanistan.

Now I'm back at the ranch in Texas, my dad in a white sleeveless t-shirt. He fought in Nam before I was born. Still strong. He looks over at the horses in the corral, a cigarette held in his large hands. I'm a child, stood by him. My dad stays there at night, watching the horses. He always does. He says it's because they're wild and free. I think it's because, deep down, he knew he never would be again. Nightmares, Nam – they put him in a cage. Loses himself to them. Never shows it to me, or mom, though. He keeps it to himself. He watches the horses till the night comes. He sits on the porch smoking these cigarettes that smell like firewood. I sit with him, tired but wanting to see my pa.

'Ya know,' he says, staring out at the night, 'I wonder about that there sun never comin back up.'

I wake up.

*

PINE OAKS, OREGON
3:30 AM

I wake up with my head spinning. I'm still drunk. I stagger out of bed - not sure why I've woken up in the first place. I realize later it is because of my dreams, but I can't put a finger on that yet. I hear loud music from next door. Synth music, like from the 80's, but modern. It's muffled through the walls. I hear a few lyrics:

'Let's take off our masks and be so natural, let's behold ourselves and break this evil spell.'

I stand up. Head hurts too much. Jesus. Feels like someone had hit me with a hammer from inside my skull. I go over to the wall, the music getting louder. I lash out – fire along my knuckles. The cracking of wood, and in the quiet of the apartment it sounds akin to cannon fire.

I put a hole through it on my side. I swear, staggering over to the sink. Misjudged my swing. Would pay for this with bruises and scars. Stupid.

I throw up into the sink. Deal with it in the morning. It can be my problem then. I stagger over to my chair, the one by the window, and hear the music slowly fade back into something manageable. I reach for the half empty bottle of whisky by the chair leg, and drink straight from it. I need to keep the shakes away. I can drink water in the morning, but for now I need to balance. Otherwise I won't sleep again. If I get it right, I won't dream. I'll just be swallowed by the dark and be gone.

I hear Christy's door open, and then a knock on mine. I ignore it. I sip it again, before taking a heartier swig that burns my heart away a little. I'm a little too far gone, but that's just fine. I don't hear next door open again, and stand uncertainly. I put a grey t-shirt on, thankful I passed out in my jeans. I head to the door, and think I hear some kind of modern version of 'Running up That Hill', same kind of synth style as the previous song. I almost admire it more. It's honest.

I peek out into the dimly lit corridor, and see Christy. She's wearing the same dress from earlier, but is sat on the floor. She's fumbling with her phone, any sobriety gone. She looks at me with unsteady eyes, and I see she's been crying a little.

'Oh, hey,' she says, closing her eyes and smiling. She rests her head against the wall. 'Sorry about the whole...uh, noise, thing. I, I kinda had a house warming. Apartment, warming. Whatever.'

'It's okay,' I say, stepping out into the light a little more. 'I was gonna call the cops. They're busy.' She smiles at me, getting the joke.

'Ah. Good for me. I got locked out.'

'Of your own apartment?'

'Yeah, fucking... Olive won't answer her phone.'

'Might be because of the music. Maybe she can't hear it.'

'Har har,' she says, fake laughing. I smile, and kneel down with my back against my own open door. She looks at me and her eyes are unfocused. I wonder if she's on drugs. Maybe.

'You want me to wait with you?'

'I, nah. It's okay, Joel. I, uh.'

I nod, before standing up. She calls to me, looking up at the ceiling. 'Wait. Yeah. I, if that's okay. I, uh. Yeah.'

'Sure,' I say, before I disappear inside to I get my whisky. I sit back down and she goes through her phone a couple times, whilst I drink silently. After a few minutes, she looks at me. Her smile is warming, illuminated in part by the cold blue of her phone screen. Jagged shadows carved into the contours of her face.

'So, I. Hey.'

'Hey.'

'I'm sorry again if we were loud.'

'It's alright. I'm off work tomorrow and aim to get blind drunk tonight anyway. No problem.'

'Sorry.'

'You've said.'

Her head rolls around, like her spine has fallen out of her skull. She looks at me from the corner of her eyes, before turning around. She pulls her knees up to her chest, and wraps her arms around herself. She rests herself against the wall and speaks again.

'I'm a shitty neighbour,' she says. I smile, taking another drink of whisky.

'Same.'

'I feel rude because we like, haven't talked.'

'Don't feel like that. It's fine. The last guy who lived in your place used to use junk and jerk off onto the hallway carpet. You're a nice reprieve.' She smiles, though I'm not sure if she thinks I'm being serious or not.

'That can't be true?'

'Yeah. Guy was called Sam. Died last year, during all that shit at Point Truth.'

'What was that?'

'Whole lot of people got shot up the road aways. Guy with an M4A1 shot the place up. Beforehand, he shot Sam. Some hooker and his dealer died here too.' She stares at me, her brow furrowed and perplexed.

'An assault rifle,' I say, and she nods.

'That's horrible. It wasn't in...In my apartment, was it?'

'No.'

'That's horrible,' she repeats.

'Yeah.' I drink more whisky, and she nods at me smiling. Still a sad gleam in her eyes, for the dead she'll never know.

'Thank you,' she says. I smile again, before wiping my face with my hand. The thunder in my head is subsiding. It'd lie in wait till morning, and then pounce. It'd kill me, one day – the accumulative one, the one that would punch a hole straight through my mind and into my soul. We're all waiting, us alcoholics, for that hangover. The last one. I wave my hand at her, try to relieve some tension.

'Nothing to thank me for. I haven't done anything.'

'I mean waiting.' Her phone pings, and she reads a text. Fingers blur as she replies. She smiles at me, standing up. I do the same. 'My friend is coming out now,' she says, and she brushes her hair behind her ear. She turns to me and smiles again, before taking a step towards me. She nearly falls, places a hand against the wall for balance. I step forward, catch her. She reeks of booze.

'I'm sorry,' she says, quietly, and she sobs a few times. She hugs me, but I don't hug her back. After a minute, I gently pat her back. I don't know what to do. Never been good with upset women. Never know how to soothe them.

'It's okay,' I say, as her door opens. Olive is stood there, her phone in her hands. She peers down the opposite end of the hallway, and then turns, seeing us. She smiles.

'Hey, how the fuck did you manage that?'

Christy looks up at me with wet, red eyes. Her pupils are like pinpricks. She leans forward and hugs me properly before turning, and Olive is looking at me with a smirk. She looks back at Christy, a wry little smile on her face.

'Well,' Christy says, 'I was going out to apologize for us being loud and stuff and then *you* closed the fucking door!'

'Christ, calm down. You're a big girl.' Olive looks at me again. 'Thanks for looking after her.'

'No problem,' I say. I turn back towards my door, and Christy waves at me. I wave back, and then close my door. I take my shirt off again, crack a window open. The night draws ever deeper into the sky, and I smoke some more. I look out of my window for an hour, before turning on the computer. I can't sleep. So I write drunk, into the night, till the day bleeds in. I don't have a name for the book yet, but know what it's about.

*

PINE OAKS, OREGON

6:30 AM

The world is a strange, surreal place. I wrote a dozen pages, though they tapered off. There was nothing of the story in them. What was saved was wanted. I take the time to throw them into the garbage, before I look at the sink I threw up into. Jesus. I sit down on the floor, my back against the fridge. I run my hands through my hair, resting my head in them. The world still spins beneath me.

I think of Alice, as I'm scrubbing puke out of the sink. I didn't dream about her, that picnic we went on. Why? I don't know.

Half an hour later, I'm drinking a glass of water and staring out at the misty streets of Pine Oaks. It had rained in the night – left a gray film in the air, the kind that looks like ghosts nuzzling up to windows. Distant mountains like the broken teeth of giants. Below, the low hum of cars. I look at the phone on the wall. I stand – legs feel gutted, boneless, tired – and stagger for it. I go over to it and punch in her cell phone number. It rings three times before I hear her speak. Her voice is sleepy, tired. I catch her mid-yawn. She worries about me, I think. I don't know why.

'Joel? Joel, is that, is that you?'

A PLACE TO BURY HORSES

I close my eyes tight. Feel my cheeks get slick with tears.
Her voice is echoing in a well in my mind. Drawing down into dark,
still waters – her voice dredges up the drowned and the dead. I see
Wyatt.

'Joel?'

I hang up. Look over to the hole I punched into the wall last
night, drunk and angry and bitter. I go over to the hole, touch the
edges of the thin wall. There are cracks and splinters growing in a
spider web all around it. I look down at my knuckles, bruised and
bloodied. Didn't notice the wound last night, too drunk. So must've
been Christy, if she didn't notice. I sigh, feeling a little of the
hangover stab into a place behind my eyes. A pulse of pain that I
have to swallow at, gulp down.

I hear a knock at the door. I turn, before heading over to it. I
rest my head against the door. I don't open it. The brass of the chain
glitters in the dawn.

'Hello?'

'Hey, Joel,' says a man I knew. I can smell cheap tobacco. I
laugh, under my breath. I look over at the clock above the newly
cleaned sink, the bucket of soapy water and rubber gloves I used still
on the floor.

'Password?'

'Tranters Creek.' I laugh. I let Gerald in, and I see he's brought donuts, and whisky. Not Ruger Rose, but still a fairly good brand. Single malt. The old man with the wrinkled, warm face the color of chocolate and intense dark green eyes smiles at me. He gives me the whisky. He keeps the donuts.

'You forget I'm coming?'

'Nah.'

'Sure. You been drinking again?'

'Yeah.'

He smiles at me. Gerald was a Vietnam Vet. A kind old man who was raised in the time of monsters burning churches and lynching. He signed on for the war his father fought – storming the beaches, freeing the men and women of different faith, hunting down monsters who slaughtered innocence in the name of the Reich. Instead, he got the jungle – the horror it brought, the morally gray. There were no monsters there, nothing that could be vilified. He never let it claw any of his soul away – not the rough growing up in the rural parts of Minnesota, or the sights he saw in Hué. He was a kind man that the world hadn't hurt. I loved him as a brother.

He takes a look at the hole in the wall, points to it. He looks at me, but doesn't say anything. He goes over to the chair in front of the TV, and then stops. He goes instead to the window, looks out over the town. I believe he is looking for a meaning as to why I am here, not moved away. Something that drew me here once and held me. But I don't know.

'How's the whole in-land thing going?'

'Good. I keep to myself still. I actually, uh...I nearly called Alice this morning. Well, I did.'

He takes one of the cigarettes from the tin he keeps in his breast pocket. Old things, that smell of dead leaves, crushed forests, and wet dirt. He loves them. I never complain. The old deserve and have earned enough in this world. He lights it up, then smiles at me, the smoke thick and heavy.

'Oh?'

'Yeah.'

'How is she?'

'Don't know. Hung up.'

'Ah. You young folks, you never know a good thing till it's gone.'

'Yeah,' I say, moving over to a reclining chair I keep for when Gerald visits. I move it next to the comfy chair, and plant my ass in it. Gerald comes over, smiling with nicotine stained teeth. I turn the TV on with the remote, and we talk. It always goes like this with Gerald – once a month, the old soldier comes over, and talks to me. We met when I got a bronze star and a purple heart.

A PLACE TO BURY HORSES

For bravery.

He shook my hand, in front of a crowd, whilst Alice cried; Wyatt sat next to her in his little suit. I hear explosions still. Since then, we stayed in touch – a care home he was supposed to be moving to in Agate, North Dakota, got hit by a bad storm last year. He decided to stay with his son in Portland. His son does admin work. I never ask what for.

The old soldier comes over to meet the younger one, to make sure he's okay.

'So, let me get this straight,' I say, laughing and smiling after a few hours. 'You and your friend, uh...Gainor, sorry, you did what?'

'We were on recon, and Gainor, he...' the old man wipes a tear from laughing, 'he falls into this river. So, we're all making sure he's okay, and he's got this leech, the size of my goddamn hand, hanging off his forehead. We burn the fucker off, obviously, but Gainor, this huge welt on his head, goes "you see that? That fucker? Nearly as big as my dick!"'

'What did you say?'

'"Makes sense. I mean, it was hangin' off your head and you gotta burn it to kill it off when it's too happy."'

He laughs, an old tired thing that reminded me of my pa when he was older and greying and getting closer to the end. A laugh that reminds me of horses on a ranch in Texas. I laugh too. Gerald coughs a few times, thick heavy things that look as painful as they sound. He leans back in the chair, places a hand briefly to his chest. He stops and lowers his hand when he notices me looking at him. I speak first.

'You okay?'

'Us folks, old soldiers, we reach our end by date when we ship off home. I'm fine young fella.' I nod.

'You want water?'

'Nah. I'd rather talk some more.'

'Okay.'

We do for a little while, and then I see it's getting to three and his son'll be outside, hoping he doesn't get shot or mugged. As I'm helping Gerald to the door, one arm around him to support him, I ask him.

'So, what ever happened to Gainor?'

'He's in Washington D.C.' I open the door, sighing once with a sad, weary smile and nodding. I knew what that meant.

'Sorry to hear.'

'It's fine. Long time ago now. I don't got no time for old troubles and ghosts, kiddo. I ain't agin' backwards.'

'Still. Sorry.'

A PLACE TO BURY HORSES

'It's fine.'

I help him down the stairs, where his son sits nervously in an expensive looking Coupe. He waves at me, looking around. He acts like he'll be assaulted any second. I wave at Gerald, and he waves back, as he drives away into the day.

There is a time, I realize, as he disappears – there will be a time that will be the last that we do this, and he would be lost as anything other than a memory. I shiver at the thought. The world was some dark hearted thing that left no one unhurt. Thresher.

No one ever gets out of life alive.

I turn around and head back into the apartment building, thinking of all the names on the black wall at Washington D.C. There is something to that monument. The way you can feel the names with your fingertips.

Over 58,000 men and boys went there to go to war. They never came home, their names emblazoned in gold upon the black stone. I think about that for a sobering time, as I climb the stairs. I think about a lot of things, but among them, always, is the way we remember the lost.

A little later, and I decide I need fresh air. Gerald always makes me need to walk. I think about a few things then too, namely Alice again. Stupid. Shouldn't have tried calling. It was dumb, and selfish. She has a new husband. A new life. I'm still trying to get over my old one. I notice rain overhead and I pull my hood over my head. I light a cigarette, before walking to the pier. Pine Oaks pier is beautiful, in its own way. Pine Oaks itself is inland, but certain people own boats they take out via the rivers that peel out to the North Pacific Ocean. Certain misty days – like today – I see the light of ships as they leave the crudely done port and go out to sea. They disappear, the lights from the cabins, into the gray. I watch them for half an hour, just simply admiring and breathing in the day. My head hurts. My eyes water for no reason, and I turn away.

I walk back into town, and up through winding streets and alleys. I don't know what belongs in them, what resides here in this part of America. I feel something pulling me towards *Robins,* but I fight it back. I don't want a drink right now, though I disagree with myself several times as I walk back along Main Street, back to the apartment building. I pass Jay on the way, sat on the sidewalk, a hat in front of him like an urchin from an old book. I toss him 5 dollars, and then carry on. He says something to me as I walk past, but I don't hear him. I see Christy stood outside the building, smoking. She looks shaken, upset. I nod at her, and she doesn't nod back. She closes her eyes instead when she sees me. I don't mind. Used to it. I'm reaching for the handle to get back into the building when I hear her.

'Hey, Joel,' she says. I turn, smiling. She's wearing a black hoody, blue skinny jeans. Sneakers, like I wore as a child. I see them all the time, though I don't understand how they're still the fashion. She smiles at me weakly, nervously.

'I, uh,' she says. The words catch in the air and hang like spiders suspended from their webs. 'I, yeah. Sorry about last night. I, uh. I was drunk. Olive said we were in the hallway?'

'Yeah. Nothing happened. I waited with you whilst she let you in.'

'I, oh. I didn't mean like that, or anything, I, uh...'

'Okay.' I turn back towards the building, and reach for the handle again. She calls me again.

'I still need to, uh, go for like groceries and stuff. Could you give me a hand later? Maybe show me the town?'

'Ask Olive,' I say. 'She'll help.'

'Olive is from Rome, up the road aways. Nearer to Portland than here, I, uh...'

'Sure,' I say. 'Knock on my door in like two hours. I'll drive us there, show you the town a little. Though you probably saw most of it last night.'

'Thanks, Joel. Super helpful. Thanks.'

'No problem,' I say. This time, she lets me go back in. I go to the apartment, and let sleep crawl over me in a wave as I collapse on my couch. I sleep for hours, not quite sure of the dreams themselves. I'm having trouble with my thoughts. I see summers live and die and winters come and the dark bleed into the day, all in my dreams.

I see my family as I arrive home, Alice's face slick with tears. She's crying, and I'm keeping her up because she keeps nearly falling. She loves me, she says; I've been gone so long. She holds me, though I noticed her hair has changed somehow. She smells different. Holds me in a warmer way. I feel the same. I'm on the crutch still at this point. I feel the weight of a medal, pinned to my uniform. I feel the air around me, the chill of it, and I miss the desert for the first time, but not the last. I see Wyatt, watching TV. The boy has no idea who I am. I've been in and out of his life for years, but he's not an infant, something born of me, no memories save the ones we remember for him later. He's his own person. He doesn't know who I am. I step past Alice, and her sister – here visiting. Her sister has a wide open mouth – she can't believe it, she says. She thought I was dead or AWOL.

No, I say, not turning as I hobble to the stranger who is my son. I just stayed in the desert.

I shake my son's hand, and Alice explains that I'm his dad. He doesn't register anything for a while, but then he hugs my legs and I feel him shiver. My heart breaks. I realize, as I fall to my knees, ignoring the pain of my wounded one, that he's holding me up. I can't stand. He has me, though. I'm not strong. He holds me up, my boy. I have never known strength as his – never will.

I'm woken up by gentle knocking on my door, and open it after getting changed to see Christy, wearing a summery dress and cowboy boots. She has her black hair tied loosely behind her head. I noticed for the first time she has one of those studs in her nose. A septum piercing, the kids call them. They remind me of what you put through a bulls snout. It's small, black metal. It adds to her features, though I still think they're strange.

'Hey,' she says. I nod, yawning. 'Did I wake you up?'

'No,' I say. 'I was just getting ready to give you the tour. Come in. Mind the mess.' I turn, heading towards the living room. I hear the door close behind me, and feel Christy's eyes on my back. I forgot about the scars. Stupid. I throw a t-shirt on, and turn. She's looked away now, I can see, but she's looking around awkwardly.

'I was hurt, that's all,' I say. She doesn't turn. I don't say anymore, apart from when she asks quietly 'what happened?'

'I was in an accident,' I say in reply, before I grab my jacket and head over to her. She looks around my apartment, her gaze catching the hole in the wall I punched in the night before. I shrug at her, embarrassed, before I speak.

'Let's get going, then. I'll drive.'

She nods, before taking a final cursory look around the apartment. She follows me then into the day, the sky beginning to take orange hues. I notice the shade of orange the sky is, a deep and dark one. Christy smiles at a woman walking her dog as we peel onto the main street.

'How was last night?'

'I, uh,' she says. 'It was fine. I feel a little rough, though. Yeah. Yeah, was good. Yours?'

'Yeah. This is the main street, where all the bars are, some stores. South of this, if you were following signs for Redmond, is Point Truth. A little west of that is a town called Rome, where your friend Olive lives, you said. But yeah. Everything starts here.'

'Those scars. They looked like they hurt.'

'Yeah. Accident. I told you.'

'Olive said you were looking after me last night. I was...I was embarrassed, earlier. When , you know, I...I kinda ignored you. I have too much, I get emotional...I'm sorry.'

'Not your fault. Booze is strange for that. Makes people act funny.'

'I just wanted to say sorry.' Christy sighs, a deep dark thing that I feel echo in the car. It came from the bottom of her soul, that sigh.

'Nothing to be sorry for.'

We pass by more streets. Signs. The trees are like giants. They tower above us, trying to stab at the sky. It all looks painted on.

'I just,' she starts to say, but she catches herself, stifling words down. I look at her for a second, before smiling and speaking.

'No one gets to make their own choices, these days. There's something wrong with everyone, wrong with America. Just try and smile a little more about it. It goes away after a while.'

I hear her laugh, a little. Just enough to know. She looks out of her window at Pine Oaks, as the store fronts bleed together in motion – the blur of a painters brush. I see something of a child in her. Inquisitiveness', a longing for something unnameable. A restlessness in her soul.

'I never thought I'd end up in Pine Oaks, you know?'

'No. I don't think a lot of the people who end up here wanted to.'

'I. I don't know.'

'You will do when you're older,' I say. She laughs again. I take her grocery shopping at the Qwick Store on Coral Street, then help her to the door of her apartment after the drive home. She thanks me, and I smile and turn to leave. I look on the TV. Half the world away, a truck filled with soldiers has hit an IED in the early hours of the morning. Their mothers and fathers and wives and husbands would receive folded flags. They will never have to know of the dark or the fire.

For a dangerous second, a long one that burns into hours, I want to get my hands on God.

The feeling passes, and in the twilight of the day I drive up to Styx Lane gun range, up near Portland. It's a little place, the range hidden in a clearing. It used to be a biker bar, or so I'm told. I half believe it. It has a feeling of violence to it that I believe was there long before the sound of brass shells hitting the floor filled the air.

There's something calming about shooting, I find. I used to go to the range a lot when I got back the last time – some kind of calm came over me, and I felt something. I struggle with that. Still.

I.

I still do.

I walk up the gravel parking lot to the sound of rifle fire. I recognise it easy enough – the choked gasp of an AR-15. Kids. They don't understand guns. They watch movies, but don't get them. Vets, if that's what I'm to be called, do.

Bob "Bones" Rueman is the owner. With his beard, tattoos, and harsh silver hair, he looks like the Hell's Angel he used to be. He's a kind, gentle man, however – never heard him swear, shout. Never even saw him on the range, save one time he wanted to show me a new .45 cal his brother got him for Christmas. He was alright at shooting. Had a bad stance at times.

'Joel, my man!' he says. He shakes my hand, pats me on the back. It's been too long, he says. We talk like old friends do. We're not, but we can pretend. He asks me if there's anything I want to try, and I say a revolver. We settle on a magnum, .357. Black metal barrel, a wooden handle. Looks like something from outer space.

He tells me it's called the Chiappa Rhino 40DS. Kicks like a mule, the rounds strong. I take second pressure, lining up sights and foresights. Squeeze the trigger. I punch a few holes in centre mass downrange, empty the cartridges after. I pick a 1911, a gun my grandfather would've used to storm the beaches of far off lands. Felt smoother, sleeker – things like this tend to age well. I almost feel remorse when I reel in the target and see that at least one shot went wide of centre. These things, they were designed to never miss. My fault, I guess. It survived a fucking war, this pistol, same as me. Yet I was the one who let it down.

I'm about to leave, my head a little clearer, when I see it on the gun shelf behind Bones. An M1 Garand.

A gun that had survived a century, still being used. The metal on it black and clear, the wood dark. I see notches on the hilt, next to the butt plate. I ask Bones what they are.

'Oh, you like her? Got used in Normandy. Picked it up in Allerdale the other day. Hear it used to be a sniper variant, M1-C.

'Course, that could be a lie. Heard the notches are kills, you know? I'm thinking more likely it's some shrapnel from, ah, Caen, maybe. Uh, Carentan. It's too random, for, you know, a knife or something.'

'Huh.'

'Wanna shoot her?'

'Yeah.'

It feels like history, as I load in the black En-Bloc clip. The bullets are the size of my middle finger – .30-06. I wonder of things, as I pull back the charging handle. Wonder of young men, sent to die in a country that had been stolen and divvied up; conquered and butchered. Beaches gave to jungle, then to desert. Still the rifle endured. Young women had their hearts broken, men became cruel, distant. Still the rifle endured. I thought of children, dying young to spare men the sins of being terrible fathers.

The rifle yet still endured.

I line up the sights, taking a careful squeeze of the trigger. Loud, violent – the things of empire. I fire a grouping of two rounds, four times. The clip flies out – a metallic ping that sounded on Bikini Atoll, on the beaches of Normandy, in the heart of the Reich as it fell. I reel in the target again with the button to the side of the range. Three of the rounds in the chest, one in the throat, and the rest in the face and forehead. Bones whistles with awe. He passes me the target, and rubs some of the gunpowder from a bullet off the paper. Wipes it on his jeans.

'Dang,' he says. 'Fucking *Saving Private Ryan* up in here.' He passes me the paper, asks if I want to shoot a couple more. I do.

Later, I'm stood on the gravel outside, Bones bringing it out flimsy plastic chairs under each arm. We sit and smoke a little. The night draws in. Bones is telling me his war stories – the time a robbery went south in a Vegas gas station, meeting the stripper who he would marry that same day, as they drove away together with him nursing a stray shotgun wound.

'Knew I had to marry Marybeth, you know? Like the night before, when I saw her.'

'This before or after her routine with the snake?'

'After, man. Definitely after.'

I smile, laugh. Smoke leaves my nostrils like I'm breathing fire from my lungs. I still hear the echo of the M1 from inside. Think it gets lost in my head. He smiles, shaking his head.

'When did you...you know? With Alice. When did you know? That you were... you were gonna marry?'

I pause.

'I never did.'

A PLACE TO BURY HORSES

I throw my cigarette onto the gravel. Stamp it out. I pat Bones on the shoulder, before driving home.

I thought of Alice, with her blonde hair, the two of us naked in her dorm at college. She rested her head on my chest in the afterglow. We used to fuck all the time, as kids do. I look in her eyes, heard the distant Arkham river as it passed by her Boston dorm room. She smiles at me, something that I feel in my heart. I kiss the tip of her nose. She smiles, kissing my chest before sighing dreamily.

'I love you,' she says, the first time. I'm young. Hadn't been to war. Seen women choke on their own blood, dying in my arms. Men's limbs severed by men with machetes. I don't know any better about how things actually are. The dark. I know not of it yet.

'I love you too.'

Back in the now, I'm startled from my thoughts by a deer and her fawn in the road, break just in time, the two of them staring at my headlights, caught in them. Can't move. I'm gasping, clenching the steering wheel. Caught me by surprise. Stupid. I remember something my Pa taught me about deer, if they get stuck staring at your headlights. I turn them off.

They run into the forest. I see them disappear into something approaching void. I take a moment. Feel my breathing slow. Heart's normal. Still beating. Fine.

A PLACE TO BURY HORSES

I drive home.

*

PINE OAKS, OREGON

7:30 PM

I think about the deer and her fawn, for a long time.
Something about it was important. Something illusory, hidden
behind it. I can't think. The rain's beginning to fall. I see a young
man, on the curb, hands raised in charity. I drive on past, as the
people on the street ignore him. I get to my apartment, drink for a
while. Look out the window to the street. I feel the kick of the rifle
still in my shoulder.

A powerful thing, that gun. It felt clear, quick, easy. The
kick, though – felt like it could move a mountain. Maybe it had been
modified, or something. Sporterized. I don't know. I see a gang of
three young men kick the homeless guy I saw earlier as I drove past.
I pretend to hold the M1 again, sat on my windowsill, and I line up
the invisible front sights with them. Bang. Chest. Blood filled lungs.
Bang. A shattered spine. Paralyzed for life. I line up the imaginary
gun with the third one as he walks away, and I realize for one
terrible moment that I'm becoming dangerous, unscrewed.
Something stormy on clear days. I lower my arms, the fake rifle
slipping from my mind. I worry then for the first time about my
drinking. I worry deeply, only to push it away.

A PLACE TO BURY HORSES

They say that battle changes you. Makes you stronger. More ferocious – a monster in the long dark of the night. Every time you pull the trigger, feel the kick, see the target fall; you are reborn into yourself, missing a shred of who you were previously. Some men don't leave the war in the desert. I didn't. I brought it home. Every time you pull the trigger. Every time.

I drink more.

I go to the bathroom, the room spinning. Look at my head, the medium-short hair there. It's too long. Won't do. I shave it off.

I don't look like me anymore, and I sleep soundly. Like when I was there, in the army. I see a little of whom I was once.

I think and dream about things I did once. Mostly, I think about the time I left Alice to join the game of war. That's what it is – win, lose. Except you don't come out clean. Every time you play you learn something more. Something that makes you cruel. Except it's more than that. Something that isn't explainable. I can't cast a stone into across the still waters of a river and explain the way it looks. We just know they skip.

Alice invites me, when I'm young, over to her house. I enlisted an hour or two before – something I bled my soul into. I was born for the army. Raised by soldiers – and not much changed when I wasn't at home anymore, either. We order pizza, watch a film I don't remember. Some old thing. Like me now.

A PLACE TO BURY HORSES

We lay on the couch together, and her head is on my chest. She's full of life still. We hadn't had Wyatt, hadn't given up on being children yet. That's what kids do, they take that. Force children to adults. To grow.

We lay there. Blissful, silent, watching a movie. I'd had a few beers with her dad, a tough mechanic by the name of Bob. Tough as nails, with a soft side – after a few too many, he'd talk about his dad. Fixing cars in the summer. Watching the sunlight strobe on their hoods. He was a good guy, Bob. Loved the booze, and I think it burnt him out in the end.

Back to then, and her head is on my chest. I feel something akin to peace, something distant, illusory – some white light piercing something grey. I close my eyes and smile. She does the same. We talk with our eyes closed facing each other for a moment.

'I'm sleepy,' she says. She yawns. I nod. My smile aches my cheeks; spirals of pain below my eyes.

'Same.'

'I don't wanna move though. You're comfy. Some kinda bed you are, mister.'

'I love you,' I say. I used to say it first all the time after she said it that once in her dorm. Then I didn't after I was a soldier, when I was back and the sand and the cordite and the sun had burnt

that part of me to coal. This was before then, though. She smiles, deeper this time, and nuzzles into my chest.

'I love you too.'

A silence. Loud. Loud enough to send a chill into me. She breaks it, thankfully.

'I love hearing your heartbeat,' she says. 'I don't want that to sound, uh, creepy, but, you know. I, uh...I...' she lets the sentence trail into a bleak warmth. I get the message.

'Guess it means I'm alive,' I say. My accent hadn't faded completely, and I still occasionally slipped into it. I was still that young guy from Texas whose father owned a ranch. I'm not now.

'Alice,' I say. She keeps her head there. I feel her stir though. There's a moment in conversation with someone you love when you can tell they're going to say something world shattering. Some kind of strange pull in your chest. Something strong. 'Alice.'

'Yeah?'

'I...I went to a recruitment thing today. I...they were advertising, you know, in town.'

'Yeah.' Her tone says the rest. I wrap my arms around her; feel her breasts on my stomach. She shivers. Something beautiful in her. It hadn't died, yet. The thing in her. The thing in me.

'I just, you know. I...my pa was in the army, my grandpa. You know, like...I...'

'You're a fucking idiot,' she says. I can't see her face but know she's crying. Feel my chest grow wet. We shiver together in the cold. After a time that stretches forward into the infinite, she looks at me. Her eyes are red, wet. Her breathing is ragged, heavy.

'Why the fuck did you do that?'

I nearly say that it's what my father did, what America has been built on. I don't. Instead, I frame her face in my hands. I love her more, in that instance, than I've ever loved myself. Such is the way of old memories.

'I'm gonna be okay, you know. I... I'll be okay.'

'So...so what happens?'

I'm crying now. A distant dawn begins to rise in the crooked corridors of my mind. I hadn't thought about Alice, my mom. Only me. Shouldn't have. Stupid. I saw something my father must've seen way back when, in my mother. When he told her when he enlisted.

'I...I applied, you know, and then I go for training, do the whole...I guess like, the exam things.'

'What about me?'

'I...'

A PLACE TO BURY HORSES

'I love you.' She cries some more. 'I love you,' she says again. I pull her close. Feel her not reciprocate, before she squeezes me back. Feels like she's squeezing the life out of me. I kiss her head.

We're silent the whole time till the end of the movie. She holds my hand, leads me upstairs. We make love, though I feel that even then she's trying to get every memory she can out of me. Like the dying of a star. An old photograph – something to keep.

I'm on top, looking down at her, and she grabs my face. Frames me. Like I was a memory, fleeting in the night. I look down into her eyes. She's crying again.

'Please,' she says, 'don't go.'

'I need to,' I say, exiting her. We lay next to each other, neither of us finished. She looks at me with red rimmed eyes.

'Why do you need to?'

'Because it's what men do, sometimes. Women, too. We, you know. We need this.'

'I'm scared.'

'Of what? Me dyin'?'

'No,' she says. She turns to me, lies on her side. I do the same. We're facing each other in the soft glow of the streetlights

~ 52 ~

outside, diffused by the curtains of her bedroom. 'I don't know what I'm scared of.'

In the now I sit on my chair. I hear the scream of the M1 echo in my head. Can't shake it. I'm scared, I realize. I'm scared of something. Like Alice, I don't know what either. I decide to capitalize. Head over to the desk, booting up the computer. I lose time, again. It bleeds together.

After a while, I stumble to bed. I stare up at the ceiling, counting my breaths. I remember a time, once, long ago, *where I did something similar.*

It was the first night I was back – Alice had put Wyatt to bed, because he couldn't settle. I couldn't either. Something had been bugging me, and I woke up with my heart racing. I look around the room, hands shaking. Takes me a second to realize I'm looking for my rifle, I can't find it, I'm panicking – and another, longer one, to realize it's not there, and never would be. I sit up, shaking. Something was different. Her hair, her smell. I reach for a packet of cigarettes on a smell bedside table to color of oak next to me. I don't smoke in the house. Not used to it. I feel Alice stir herself awake. She talks to me in a haze, drunk from sleep. I look at her shadowed form in the dark. A little of the moonlight carves dark shadows on her face – half of her is bathed in milky blue light. She looks like someone had painted her into existence – some mournful thing born of the moon.

A PLACE TO BURY HORSES

'Joel? Joel, what's wrong?'

I look at her, silent. I look around the quiet room. The desert is far away. I am happy to be home – it just doesn't feel all too much like mine anymore. It's hard to explain. Alice puts her arms around me.

'Joel?'

'You feel different,' I say. I stare at the wall. I feel Alice tighten her grip, but she doesn't say anything at first. A moment goes by, then another. A troop of them march by.

'What do you mean?'

'I...' I wince. Turned my leg too quick. Still not healed right. Pain splinters through a shattered bone – like vines of fire. I exhale sharply, and then try again.

'I...you, did you...I...the way you hold me. I don't, I don't know. It feels like you...like...'

'Hey,' she says, quietly. Whispers. She places a hand on my face, gently, and kisses me. Her other hand runs through my hair. 'It's still me,' she says. I nod. Close my eyes. Count to four.

'You know that, right? That, I, I'm here? Wyatt's here? We're, we're a family.'

'I know. I'm sorry. I just...I noticed, is all. You, you just held me different, I think. I'm sorry. I'm stupid.'

A PLACE TO BURY HORSES

'*No, Joel, hey. No. Leave it. It's okay. We're fine. I love you.*'

'*I love you too.*' *The dark is shook away by the opening of the bedroom door. The hallway light bleeds in. Wyatt stands there, knuckling his eyes. He yawns. I put the cigarette back on the table, and swing my legs out of bed. I look at him for a moment. I don't know what to say. Alice, thankfully, speaks to the child. My child. Because I don't know what to say.*

'*Hey, sweetie. Hey. What's wrong?*'

'*I had a bad dream and can't find Mr. Bear.*' *I look at the child. He looks at me – I see now his eyes are red. He's been crying. How long had he been there, in the dark, alone? Before coming to us? I don't know. I run a hand through my hair. I stand up.*

'*I'll, uh. I'll help you find your bear.*'

Wyatt doesn't say anything, but nods. I stand up, and smile at Alice. She looks at me like I'd fallen off the moon. Feel like I have. Wyatt goes to his room, and halfway there I feel his tiny hand wrap around my wrist. I look down at him, and he stares ahead with red eyes. His bedroom is decorated in Dinosaur wallpaper, toys. I notice a sugar skull, though, on a bookshelf covered in DVD's. I nod to it as Wyatt crawls back into bed.

'*Hey, what's, uh...what's that?*'

'*My friend Alexa got me it. She says it's a good luck thing. I don't know.*'

'Mexican?'

'Yeah. Her family came over a long time ago.'

'Oh.' I look at the sugar skull, smile. Then I remember one time I saw a man have half his face blown off by weapons fire at a car checkpoint. He had sped up on approach to us, in those early days – we ordered him to stop, and he didn't. Part of me wondered whether or not he even understood what we were saying. The man had a pregnant woman in the backseat, in labour. He was trying to rush through to get her to hospital. Instead we tore them apart with automatic fire and close groupings. I shiver. Human skulls don't look like the sugar ones; not really.

I turn away, trying not to think about it anymore. I sit on the edge of the bed, run a hand through Wyatt's hair. It's like mine, a little. I smile.

'So, this, uh...Mr Bear.'

'He's my friend.'

'That's good.'

'I don't know where he is. He's a really good bear though.'

'That's even better.'

I stand up, look around. I guess I'd know it when I saw it. I look under the bed and see him – an old looking thing, a brown smiling bear. I remember, now. I gave him this as a baby. It's old, worn slightly. Wyatt speaks to me as I reach under the bed.

'Watch out for the monster under there, be careful.'

'Oh, don't worry about me. I'm friends with all the monsters. Besides...' I reach for the bear, pull it out gently. Wyatt laughs and extends his arms. He gives the bear his hug. '...He doesn't look like a monster.'

'Thank you.'

'You are more than welcome, young man.' I look at the bear and smile again. Such old things. Me and him both. I feel calm, but there's still something there. I look around the room. Wasn't here for any of it.

'Are you my dad? Like, for real?'

'Yeah. I, ah. I've been at work. Long time. I, uh, got hurt. So I get to stay here now.'

'Okay. Matty Sourley from school never met his dad. I didn't know if I was like him, or not.'

'No. I promise.' I feel something heavy in my chest, something cool like a dark stone. 'If you'll have me.'

'Yeah.'

'You want me to leave the light on?'

He nods. I stand up, stretching. I feel the bones and pins in my leg. I think about the AK round that, almost a year ago, nearly cost me it. Six months PT. Honourable discharge. I look at the sugar skull again.

I turn to Wyatt, who has buried his face into Mr. Bear.

'You know, monsters hate the daylight. They're scared of it. I think that's kinda sad. So, you shouldn't be scared of them. They don't get to play outside with their friends or anything. They just get cranky.'

'Oh. That's kind of sad.'

'I know. So, that's why they like to stay under beds, and in houses. They like to be around people, otherwise they'd be lonely.'

'Oh. I guess that's okay. Maybe they want to have Mr. Bear for the night?' Wyatt begins to put the bear back under the bed, and I laugh and smile and speak to him.

'It's okay. I asked if you could keep him. They said they're okay.'

'Oh. Tell them thank you.'

'I will do.'

'Goodnight Dad.'

'Good night. I love you, Wyatt.'

'I love you too.'

I close the door, not all the way. Just leave a sliver of it open. I smile at the boy, and then head back into the bedroom. I see Alice is asleep. Peaceful. I leave her. I sit on the sofa in my living room, look around. Subtle changes. A new TV. I think the couch is new, but don't remember.

It's like I'd stayed still in the ocean, and everyone and everything else had flowed past. I wasn't all the way here. I fall asleep on the couch.

Dark.

*

PINE OAKS
5:30 AM

I smile as I think about that old bear. My dream is of that moment. I wake up smiling. Wyatt. My boy. I don't think about medals, or stories of war. I don't think about Alice, or Christy. I don't think about anyone.

Just Wyatt, offering a monster his teddy bear so it wouldn't be alone. I find something beautiful in that. In what he could've been. Could've. Should've.

Because of me, I won't ever know. I go for a walk. My leg still twinges, but it's manageable – a barely there ache to remind me of where I've been. I see stars burning away by the coming of the dawn. Hear the Wagnerian calls of sirens pierce through the streets.

It's about 7:30 when I'm home, and I see Christy getting out of a car. The same car as before, wearing gym gear. Her face is pale, bone white. She is carved of sickly alabaster. Mascara has run as though she's been crying. She regards the car as it drives away, and I'm walking slower towards the door. She runs a hand over her face, before she notices me. Eyes downcast - ashamed. I stop walking, trying to read her face. She's crying again, but trying to smile. She wipes tears from the corner of her eyes. I nod at her, and then cross the street. She closes her eyes, and shakily reaches for a packet of cigarettes in her gym bag. She closes it quickly when I reach her, and smokes with shaking hands.

'I, uh...'

'Hey,' I say. 'Meant to rain later.'

She smiles, knows what I'm doing. Taking her mind off everything.

'I... Is it?'

'Yeah. Pretty heavy. Rolls in down the mountains. It's actually kinda nice, especially at Pine Oaks pier.'

'We have a pier?'

'Yeah. Overlooks a lake that reaches the sea, through rivers and creeks. Sometimes boats come in to moor for a time.'

'Oh.'

'Do you want to go?'

She looks at me. I can't read her face. She smiles, with a little sadness at the edge. I want to put a hand on her shoulder. Tell her the world isn't all dark. I can't do that, though. I don't believe it enough myself. I will never lie to her.

'I...yeah,' she says. 'I'd like that.'

'Good. Great. I, uh, I have work at ten until six. Then we'll go?'

'Sure.'

I look at the dawn. It peeks over the mountains to shed light on the lost people like us. Adrift. Her hands are still shaking. She stares at the sun as it hides behind dark clouds. I do the same.

She wipes her face again. Eyes are bloodshot. She smiles, before casting a glance down the street to the car she had gotten out of. It slowly fades away into the distance. I wonder who was in the car.

'I'm not a whore,' she says. Her voice cracks as she does so. I look at her with a frown. I nod. I see a young woman here, scared of something – at the moment, of being judged.

'Neither am I,' I say, trying to smile. I think I about manage it, because she laughs.

'Fuckin' asshole,' Christy says under her breath. She shakes her head. I see a thousand yard glare wash over her eyes. She stares into the distance. I worry that damage has been done.

'Do you want me to stay with you?'

'I, nah. It's okay. Um, so can you like just knock when you're ready to, ah...show me where the boats are, I guess?'

'Sure.'

I start to head towards the door to the building when I turn and speak to her.

'Christy, please smile. Even just for a little bit. Even just for a minute, for yourself. Okay?'

'I...' she starts to say, eyes wide. There's no words, I guess; so she nods and smiles with a little warmth. Her eyes say, jokingly, *there you go.*

I nod. 'Thanks,' I say.

I get showered, get ready for work. The routine is almost thoughtless. I put the news on whilst I'm drinking coffee, listening. Greg Slaugh – the puppet from *Thunderbirds* – was talking about the drug *White Claudia* again. It's getting traction, that stuff; in the last few months – lots of kids dying of it. I turn the news off, sighing. Sometimes, there's too much in this world.

I think about that the whole time I drive to work.

*

When I get there, Liv smiles at me like I hadn't seen her smile before. She looks...different. Happy. I think that's what it is, something happy. I'm not complaining – if anything, it's refreshing to see someone I care about genuinely positive. It fills you with a kind of warmth. *Finally,* it says, *things are working out.*

'Morning, Joel,' she says. Looks up from the screen. She smiles, a little puzzled. She points to her head, then touches her hair.

'You've...uh. You've lost some...hair, there.'

'I know.'

'It suits you,' she says. She goes back to the screen, her smile a little curve at the corner of her mouth.

'You seem in a good mood,' I say. 'Three hundred percent, definitely in a good mood.'

'Oh, yeah. I ah, I am. I...well, I was thinking. About, well, life, you know?'

I walk over to the reception and cross my arms on it; lean forward.

'Are you okay?' I ask.

'Yeah,' she says, smiling. 'I was kinda wondering if maybe you'd like to get a drink?'

I don't expect that. It throws me off.

'I...uh...'

'I'm sorry,' she says. She's blushing a little, just enough to tell. 'I, ah, I just wondered, is all.'

'I...yeah, okay. Sure. I'll...I'm, I'm busy tonight, got a thing with a friend. Tomorrow? We can go for something to eat. Yeah?'

'Sure,' Liv says. She looks down at the computer, starts typing away. She still talks to me, though.

'I'll, um, do you want to book a place, or, or should I?'

'Oh Christ, I don't know. I'm a little out of the whole...um...dating, thing. Haven't in a while. You pick a place. Just, ah, text me the address and I'll drive us,' I say as I turn to leave.

'Okay. Hey, uh, Joel?'

'Yep?'

'Um...thank you.' Liv smiles again shyly, like she'd been invited to prom by the high-school king. I smile and chuckle a little, before heading to the IT Lab. The kid is there again, the one who was taking notes from dusty books. I see him with his brow furrowed, looking at something hastily scrawled with handwritten notation. I make a curious involuntary smile and he looks at me. He nods at me, and puts down the paper. Pinches the bridge of his nose, between thumb and forefinger. The book on the table, the one he's making notes on, is called *The Theory Of No Man – An Encyclopaedia of Pessimism in the Modern Day.*

'Tired?' I ask.

'Yeah,' he says. Smiles, laughs once under his breath. 'Yeah, I, ah, yeah. Late nights.'

'Oh?'

'Yeah. I'm doing, ah, school work. I, you know, leave it too late all the time.'

'I rememeber those days.'

'Really?'

'A little. Too old for the specifics. Well, I'll letcha back to it.'

The kid nods, and moves back to the writing of notes and occasional glances to books. I do a few more rounds, before getting water from the cooler. Head's starting to hurt again. The thunder of drums. I sip water and stare out of the window. The rain I talked about with Christy earlier begins to fall. Batters down at the windows like a ship in a storm.

I finish my shift, soldiering through the slowly spreading fire behind my eyes that put stars in front of them. I never see the other guard. Always wonder about that. Pass Liv on the way.

'Hey, so, uh, yeah. Tomorrow?' I ask, pulling on my coat from the coat rack in the reception hub.

'Yeah. I'll, ah, I'll drop you a text. Pass me your phone.'

I do, and see her fingers type into the keypad. She passes me it back, her number entered in. I saved it.

'Drop me a call, ah, if you want?'

'Sure, Liv. I gotta get.'

'Later, Joel.' She smiles at me warmly, but I'm already halfway to the door to return the favour. I step into the rain, stare into the dark above. It's cold out. The kind of cold that places fingers of ice on your bones. I shiver, light a cigarette, and walk to my car.

*

It's stopped raining when I get home. Thankful for that – I see the warm glow of the apartment building windows, and for a moment I almost feel like it's somewhere I want to be. The moment passes as I pull into the garage to the side, drop my car off and lock it tightly. I walk into the building, head to my room. Jay is on the stairs, staring into nothing. I nod at him, and he ignores me. I swear I smell the burnt, sickly smell of heroin as I walk past. I feel for Jay sometimes. Then I remember people make their own ghosts and monsters, and I stop feeling that way for a while.

I head to my room, change. I go outside, taking a passing swig of whiskey to get rid of the headache a little. It works, and I walk to Christy's room, knock three times. I hear nothing, and a purple light bleeds out under the door.

I knock again; I'm halfway turning to leave when I hear her call from inside the room.

'Hey, Joel, ah, just come in!'

'I,' I say to the door, 'are you sure?'

'Yep!'

I nod, and walk in. The room is strange – lit by a purple neon sign held on a brick wall. The image is of a pin-up girl – the kind seen on posters from the fifties. Over by the kitchen – because it's laid out the same to mine, I know where to look – are what appear to be pots of herbs. Sage, thyme. Things to cook with, to share with someone. I smile. The place looked like it had fallen out of a Brooklyn Flea Market sale.

Christy was sat on the couch, pulling on black boots. She turns whilst struggling with putting her left one on. Her smile is happy, if a little breathless.

'Oh, ah, hey! Sorry, I, ah, I had a nap.'

'It's okay,' I say. I take another glance around the room. 'It's alright.'

'Huh,' she says, as she stands up. She rubs her hair on either side of her head, so it has volume. 'And we're good,' she says. I smile.

I walk with her down the street to the pier, seeing signs for the 4th of July festival. It's always pretty special, so I hear. I never go, though. Something about the gunpowder smell, or maybe the noise. Maybe.

'So how was your day?' she asks. She looks in the windows of stores as we go past.

'Ah, uh, not that bad. Work. Yours?'

'I...I think so. Yeah. I called my parent's up, *that* was pretty strange. Not talked in a while, you know?'

'Yeah.'

'You, ah, speak to your parents?'

'I...nah.'

'They okay?'

'Yeah,' I lie. 'We just don't talk much anymore. You know, um, I don't really have the time.'

We pass by Orchard Lane, by the *Littlerock Cafe,* when Christy laughs a little under her breath. 'Things are named funny in this town,' she says.

'Compared to where?'

'I don't know. Texas, really.'

'You're from Texas?' I ask. I feel something. I was always a Texan at heart.

'Yeah. Austin. You?'

'Ah, a little ranch near June.'

'I think I have a cousin who lives there,' she says, as I begin to see the pier loom into view from the dark. At the end of the wooden platform that makes the pier up, I see a boat with the lights on, a little fishing thing. These things make no sense – travelling their slow crawls to the sea. Moor there – Portland isn't that far. They come here though, all the same. I see Christy smile from the corner of my eye.

'Woah. I thought, uh, wow. A boat. Um, why do, ah, why do people come here?'

'I guess fishermen who can't afford to moor in Portland follow the rivers down and come here.'

'Cool,' she says, lighting a cigarette. The roses on her hand, briefly, are illuminated in a neon-chilled blue from a liquor store window. The smoke is a blue haze that bleeds from her mouth.

'It's a boat on a lake, but yeah,' I say. I do the same. Mine is dimly lit by the streetlight we pass under. We walk to the edge of the pier, passing an Ice-cream stand I rarely see open anymore. It was built in the sixties, so I'm told by the sign next to it. There's a bench there, right at the end; near the fence that covers the edges of the platform. I sit down on it, and she stands by the railing. My leg hurts. Aches old and new coming in like the tides around us.

'Woah,' she says. She smiles like a child would do, staring at the single boat on the lake as it floats, gently, to the river to carry it slowly to sea.

In many ways, she is still a child, I think to myself. I smile and stand up, taking my place by her side. She looks at her phone for a minute, before placing it in her leather jacket's pocket. I fold my arms over the railing. The smell of rainwater on the wood. She does the same.

'How long do you stay here?' She asks me, watching the boat become a floating ghost of light, hidden by the night.

'Sometimes a couple hours. Just, you know. Sometimes.'

'I can see why.' She smiles, runs her free hand through her hair, pushing it behind her ear. I notice, now, she has another tattoo – a love heart, tiny and pink and faded, inside her ear.

'That must've hurt,' I say. I laugh; feeling a twinge of how mine felt long, long ago. She turns to me for a second and touches her ear, before laughing a little and turning back to the fading boat.

'Oh, yeah. Low impulse control as a kid.' She looks down at the dark waters of the lake, and closes her eyes smiling. 'I forget I have it, sometimes.' I nod, smiling. We watch the boat go to out to sea. Fade away. We go back to *Rosie's,* and Christy buys me a beer. I let her, but stop her at one.

We talk for a while, about things friends do. We're both smoking, and she's wearing my jacket over her shoulders as the cold frosts the windows of cars parked on the road. Streetlights create strobes on the hoods of passing cars as we walk together. It's midnight, or near enough.

'So,' she says, 'that was... It was nice. Thanks, I mean. Uh.'

'I agree. Thanks to you too. I don't...I don't do this often. At all.'

For a strange moment I think about the man who used to live next door to me. Never would find out if the junkie who used to live in there could've turned things around. Before a bullet punched a hole in him, and his life bled away.

'Joel?'

I realize I zoned out. I shake my head, smile at her.

'Sorry, uh, I was, ah. Sorry. Someplace else.'

'It's alright.' Silence stretches in front of us for a good ten feet, and when we get to the other side she speaks to me.

'So, um...do you, ah, do you have a girlfriend, or anyone? Like, they're cool with us hanging out, right?'

'I...well, no. I don't. I have a date, maybe, or something, tomorrow night, but, um. No. No girlfriend. I was married though,' I start to say, but catch myself. I bite back the rest of the sentence. Stupid.

'Oh?'

'Yeah, once.'

'Oh, um...I'm sorry, Joel. That sucks. I, you know, ah. I was going to, at one point, with this...this guy, but um, we never, never got around to...um...did I say I was sorry?'

'You did,' I say with a weak smile. *Wyatt, his face twisted in pain. I feel rain on my face, feel blood on my back. The windscreen is in shards. Crystalline stars. Alice cries in the night.* I close my eyes. Christy places a hand on my shoulder, gently, tentatively.

'Hey,' she says, but then struggles. 'Hey, it's, it's...it's alright. What, what happened if you don't mind me asking?'

'I...it doesn't matter.' She nods. Before I know it, she's hugging me from the side, awkwardly.

'Hey, big guy. Don't worry.' A pause, then she adds 'I just realized how tall you are. Shit, dude.'

I smile a little and nod. She lets go after a moment, and I look at her. She smiles brightly and closes her eyes. We carry on walking and reach the building. I walk her to her door and she passes me my jacket, smiling.

'We should do that again, if you, uh, if you want,' she says, and I nod. The purple light from the sign in her apartment bathed the underneath of her door in an eerie glow, like a pagan ritual to an old, dead God gone awry.

'Yeah, I would.'

'I'm sorry, uh, I didn't mean to, um, upset you. I don't have a filter sometimes, and, I, uh, I...'

'It's fine. You didn't know,' I say. I place a hand on her arm gently. 'You didn't know.' I nod, and go to my own apartment. I'm fighting memories the whole time – things I don't want to remember but do. I get into the apartment, lock it, and place my back against the door – I slide against it so I'm sat on the floor. I look at my hands, rested on my knees; the bruises from where I'd punched a hole in the wall the other night still fresh, healing slowly. Both my hands are shaking. I close my eyes, clenching my fists like I'm trying to crush stones in them. Wyatt's final moments in pain. I shiver, clenching my fists tighter. I feel rainwater through the windscreen. I feel like I'm drowning, for a moment.

I go to the fridge, try to get a beer out, but my hands won't stop shaking so I stop trying. I sit on the floor. Count to four slowly, breathing in through my nose. Out slowly through my mouth. I spend the majority of the night like this. I feel like I'm dreaming while awake the whole time.

*

PINE OAKS
6:00 AM

I get to work the next day early, happy. I'd wrote a little more of my own book before sleeping – not enough to be happy, but enough to know I was doing something. Felt a spark of something akin to pride in that. I have the feeling fleetingly, sparingly. Enough to know I've earned it.

Liv isn't at the reception. Marty is; an old man with knees and knuckles made of painful, hot glass. He sometimes acted as a custodian. I think deep down he just wants to be alone like a dog on their last legs.

'Marty, hey,' I say. He reaches a shaky hand out, and I take it gently. His skin feels like tissue paper. I think a breeze would do some damage to him, he's so frail.

'Ah, Joel,' he says, 'how are you my boy?'

'I'm, you know. I'm good. Where's Liv?'

'She, well. She called in sick, today. Poor thing sounded ill.' I nod. I wander around books for a time, go to the IT lab. The young man is there, still making up for lost time – *aren't we all*, I say to myself and the world. I call Liv on my lunch, get voicemail. Twice. I'm halfway through hanging up the third time when she picks up.

I've been around a woman with heartbreak in her. Liv sounds like someone had cut her heart out.

'Hel-hello?'

'Liv? Joel. How are you? Marty said you were sick.'

'I, um. I. Yeah. I'm, um, I'm sick.'

A beat. I see a police car drive past, sirens blaring. It rounds a corner and disappears.

'Liv, are you okay?'

'Y-y-yeah. Why?'

'You're crying.'

'I'm, I. I'm fine, Joel. Really.'

'I...'

'Look I gotta go. Um, can, can we rain check tonight? I, I just, you know. Um. I'm sick.'

I'm hardly surprised. Feel stone walls around my heart. Count to four in my head.

'Sure, no problem. See you tomorrow?'

'Yeah...yeah. Yeah, Joel. I'll, um, I'll see you later.' She hangs up; the line goes into a monotone ring. I close my eyes, letting the sound ring in my ears for a short time.

I finish up work and go for a drive. I don't know where. I go through the woods around Pine Oaks – part of me wants to go to Point Truth, visit the memorial there, but I don't. I can't think. Can't think at all. So I just drive around, till around eleven. The rain is like bullet casings on my windshield, the moon a silver coin.

I pull up outside the apartment to see Christy with her gym bag. She's shivering in the rain, her hands wrapped around herself. I drive forward a little, and open my window.

'Are you okay?'

'No man,' she says, looking at her phone. She looks up and down the street after. 'My fucking cab is late, and I'm late already and...'

'Hop in.'

'Joel, I, I can't, I...'

'I don't care what you do for a living,' I say. I look at a traffic light, changing to green from the amber. 'What I do care about is someone freezing to death outside my apartment.'

She looks down the street, towards a road that bled into forests, night, and more rain.

'Oh, oh fuck,' she says, and she walks briskly around to the passenger side door. I roll the window up, and she gets in. I feel the cold from a seat over. She throws the gym bag into the back, and I put the heater up. She shivers more. Soaked to the bone.

'Are you alright?'

'I...Joel, I don't know. I don't know about this.'

'Where are we going? You shouldn't worry so much. Adds years to you.'

She doesn't say anything to me, merely stares out at the Chinese restaurant across the road. The sign bathes us both in blood red neon. I nod, lighting a cigarette up. I tap her gently on the shoulder, and she takes one. She has a lighter already, and soon the two of us are filling the interior with smoke.

'Where am I going?' I ask.

'If...if you go this way towards Rome, um, I'll tell you when. Okay?'

'Sure.' We drive a little forward, only a few yards, when she puts the radio on. Betty Lake talking about those things she did. The two of us, only a little more than strangers, driving in the rain and the dark. Betty speaks like the jazz singers of old. Jessica Rabbit, mixed with heroin. Sultry, strong, delicate.

'...It's like we already know, right? These things we do...It's enough to make a person scream at the night. Ain't that right, beautiful people? The night...well, you can blame the night for everything, if you try hard enough. Just don't look at it for too long though...you might see yourself. This next one is by a couple of real smooth folks from Portland; *Cromarty High* with...*Amy.*'

Jangly, ethereal music fills the car. The forest stretches ever above us, and the rain falls hard. A part of me feels like, one day, it might rain forever. Not tonight, but maybe one day.

'Im sorry if I seem...a little...uh. You know. I just, I...'

'You're my neighbour. I wouldn't worry. Cold like this with the rain. Wouldn't leave you out there.'

'Thanks, Joel.'

The car is filled with ambience like something The Cure would have written once. The guy and the girl both sing at the same time, as guitars and pianos create walls of sounds.

"Now there was a new me; with my arms outstretched, we'd withstand almost anything."

'I like them,' Christy says, staring out at the forests. I nod.

'Reminds me of the stuff I used to listen to,' I say.

'Joy Division fan? Reminds me of them, a little.'

'Nah. Well, a little. Good music fan.' Christy smiles, the first one I've seen her let go since she got in the car. I smile at her, and playfully jab her in the arm. She turns, mock surprise playing across her features, before she wipes a hand down her face to get rid of a little of the rain.

'Um... Joel, I know I kinda like, ask the wrong stuff, like, all the time...I swear, I think I'm like, on the spectrum...Which I'm working on...um, aren't you supposed to be on a date?'

'Yeah. Uh, she was, she. She's sick. So, you know.'

She points to the roof of the car, the rhythmic sound of the storm like drums creating texture over the track on the radio. As she speaks, she winks sarcastically.

'Rain-check?'

'Oh my God,' I say, laughing. 'You tell jokes like...well, jokes my grandparent's wouldn't even like.'

We both laugh, only a little. The radio plays on. I pass a sign for Rome, Oregon, and Christy starts to squint through the windshield and the deluge. She sighs, before closing her eyes and gently placing a hand on my arm.

'Um, its...if you just go up the ways, um, there's a road by the highway to Rome. Um, it cuts through some trees, goes through open fields. Just...uh...you're following signs for "The Pearl Palace."'

I nod. Suddenly, things click. Stripper. I nod, smiling. She looks out at the night, and I hear her sigh again. Shame radiates off her, like she was born of it and was never once a young person, making mistakes like the rest of us do.

'So, you...um...'

'Yeah. I, you know. I, I just need some cash while I...well, um, while I sort out some things, you know. At home.'

'Right.'

She looks at me with sad delicate eyes; and I look back at her with a weak smile. What I thought was true, when we first met – she did have too big of a heart, too much love. She wouldn't keep it, not for long, not here. I see the first sign for The Pearl and follow it through a small clearing. I see it.

The building in a way resembled every other dive-bar I'd ever seen – a low roofed, slightly higher than ground level squat of brick and wood. Outside, a tough looking guy in a black t-shirt and a head with a haircut so severe you could see the lines of his skull stood smoking. He looked up at the night once and swore. The sign for the places was a string of pearls, resting just above a pair of breasts.

I clench my jaw a little. Never felt comfortable, places like this.

I look at Christy, though; and I rememeber she's a scared girl who is already upset at what she does. Push my feelings aside. Think about her.

'So, you needing a ride back?'

'No, I, uh...Tony, he'll, um, give me a lift.'

'Tony?'

'My boss.' She smiles at me, and for a minute, I think she believes that everything is fine. She reaches into the back seat as she speaks, and takes the gym bag.

'I'll be okay, honestly. Go home, I'll, you know. See you later.' A moment of hesitance, then she kisses me on the cheek once.

'Thanks for the lift, big guy,' she says. She steps out into the night, and I watch her disappear into rain and neon. The tough guy nods at her, and I see him through the windshield. He gives me the thumbs up, and throws his cigarette into the dark. I stare at him while he follows Christy in. My hands shake a little again. I stare at the place, this Babylonian neon drenched nightmare. All I think about is the girl who just went in there. I sit in the dark for a time.

*

It's even darker by the time I get back. I sit in my car outside, smoking. The rain hasn't let up yet. I look at the street lights, signs. I wait, for a while.

In the Army, you wait a lot. A lot more than you'd think. 90-95% is the kind of boredom where it can do damage on its own. Then there's the other 10-5%, where you sometimes see or do things that settle in your bones and burn photographs into your mind. I close my eyes. *In my mind I wrap my arms around Alice, in winter, whisper the word "love" in her ear. Snow is all around us, in Forest Park in Portland.*

I open my eyes, and shiver. I get out of the car and stand in the rain, before taking a step to the apartment block. I freeze. Not yet. I can't. Too much is playing in my head – need to dull it. I head to *Rosie's*, instead. I pass the homeless man who got beat up, his face swollen and raw. I pause in the rain, and he looks at me with his hands outstretched.

'You got anything, man? I just need a little, you know, to get a hotel, or, or...'

'You shouldn't fucking lie,' I say, though I don't know where it comes from. I'm taken aback by how blunt I am. Shake my head. I give him five bucks and head past him. I don't know whether I was saying that to myself, or to him. *Rosie's* is quiet when I get there, and I take my usual spot by the bar. Sarah is wiping down the counter, talking to a couple of the other regulars. I wave at her, smile. She does the same. I notice something, then, but I don't mention it. There, on her wrists. Something akin to a raw tally, only just healing. She's young.

'Jesus fucking Christ,' I say, lowering my head. I run a hand through my stubbly hair. I'm interrupted by my quiet thoughts of unease by Sarah, smiling and beaming like she wasn't a girl who hurt herself.

'Howdy there. Didn't even recognize you with the whole buzz cut.'

'I...' Don't look at her wrist. Don't. She'll know.

'I, you know, wanted a change.' I smile at her, or try to. I don't break eye contact. Can't.

'Well, I preferred the semi-perm, not gonna lie. Got a real strong, like, ABBA vibe from the curls.'

'It'll grow back.'

'Usual?'

'Yeah.' She smiles and turns, beaming. I follow her with my eyes before lowering my gaze. I close my eyes, shake my head again. I look around the bar, and see Liv.

She's sat on her own, far down the bar in a booth. She has a hood up, but I can see it's her. I recognize her, like you can do with people. She stares, listlessly, at the bottom of a wineglass in front of her on the table. The bottom has faint, light red liquid still in it. Watered down blood. Sarah puts the whiskey in front of me, and I smile.

'Hey, is she okay?'

'I, ah...' Sarah leant forward. Don't look at her arms, the thin lines visible just at the end of her sleeves. 'Well, she looks pretty beaten up, but um...'

Sarah shrugs.

'It sucks, you know? I don't wanna, you know, say anything, but, uh...'

'Thanks,' I say. I stand up. Beaten up. It puts a ringing in my ears as I walk towards her at the booth, tentatively. I take a sip, and Liv looks surprised when she sees me. Her eye is swollen, and black. I don't say anything at first, but sit down in front of her.

'Oh, God,' Liv says. She wipes her other eye of a tear.

'What happened to you?'

'Nothing, I, I, uh,' she starts to say. I sip the whisky again and cut her off.

'What happened?'

'I...' Liv sighed. I reach across the booth, and gently lift her hood up. She lets me.

Her face. Her left eye was swollen shut, her nose bruised. Lip cut. Cheek cut. I feel something in me move. I cock my head a little. She turns away, so her bad eye isn't visible.

'I...my, my ex. He's, you know...he's a good guy, he just, he...gets angry.'

So do I, I say to myself. I don't know what I'm doing. I feel my breathing go shallow. It's like in the desert. I take a deep, sobering breath. I don't know what I'm doing, but my trigger finger twitches against the glass with no rhythm.

'Joel, it's okay, I, I kept his, his mothers ring, and, I didn't want to...'

'I don't care. Where is he?'

'Joel?'

'Where is he?'

'Joel, I...I don't think you should do that. It's, it's you know, it's okay. I'm okay.'

'Where is he.' I feel my face grow red. Breathing's shallow again. Exhale. Finger twitch. Second pressure. *The scream of an M1 on Normandy.* I pinch the bridge of my nose with thumb and forefinger.

'I...Joel, you're scaring me.'

'Why the fuck would you let him do that to you?'

'I...Joel, I...'

'Call the cops. Get angry. Hurt him. Don't just sit there.'

'Joel...' she says. Her voice is a little louder now.

'You, me, everyone, everything always goes wrong, and no one ever does a fucking thing,' I say. My temper flares. Feel like a Minotaur with my nostrils flaring. I slam the whiskey on the table top. Sarah looks over from the bar. Liv whispers to me, as I lean back. I raise my hands up to Sarah, before drumming them gently on the table.

'Joel...'

'Hey, Joel,' Sarah says to me from the bar, 'I think, that, um...Maybe, you should go.'

I nod, but stay sat down. Breathe. Exhale. Slow. Unclench your hands. Stop the blood boiling. I look at Liv and see she's crying. I close my eyes before standing up. I leave half my whiskey. Don't need it. I speak to Sarah as I leave into the rain. I don't know what I'm doing. Embarrassed.

'Sorry.' I don't know whether I believe it myself or not. I can pretend to.

I go home, and write, but only for half an hour. I'm restless. I stand by the window all night. I'll call in sick, tomorrow. I want to go to the range again, just...just to feel the recoil again. I sit on the window sill and smoke.

Christy turns up, just after 5:00 in the morning when the sun has beaten back the night and the sky is aflame. She looks haggard, more than she has done any other time. I see a weight in her heart. She walks with a limp, this time. I look down at her, with my body tired but my mind *filled with gunfire*. It's almost like I'm not really there – something illusory. A magician could wave his hands and I'd disappear in a cloud of smoke.

Christy looks up at me, her face pale. In the rain, she appears as something from mythology. There is a quiet moment of understanding, in that dawn. It travels from her to me.

I see tears in her eyes and her makeup has run down her face like a ghostly bride from a Victorian horror tale. I'd wager that last night was the longer kind. She folds her arms as the black car drives away. She shivers a few times, and I see her sit down on the step. I think of going outside, but I don't. I go to the chair, and fall into something like slumber – I still hear everything, but I shut down. Can't explain it. Can't.

*

PART TWO:

BLACK ARROWS

PINE OAKS, OREGON
10:30 AM

I stand outside of Christy's room. I smell cigarette smoke under her door. I'd called in sick half an hour ago – said I must've caught what Liv had. Didn't feel well. I lift my arm up to knock, but don't; instead I place my forehead against the wood, and slide down it. I'm sat down with my back against the door, staring at the wall. I sigh, and close my eyes. Place my head in my hands and wipe my face. The window to the street lets in golden hues as the day shines down on Oregon. I talk to the door, knowing she can hear me. I hear her crying, after all; the wood too thin.

'Alice left me,' I say. I don't know why. I blink a few times, heavy fast things like the beating of wings. 'I, I made a mistake, once.'

I hear gentle, soft footsteps, the sounds of crying. I hear Christy slide to the floor like I am, opposite side of the door. I hear her breath smoke out, exhaling sharply in bursts *like shrapnel or gunfire*.

'I'm, people do these things. They don't know why. I don't. Are...are you okay?'

'No,' she says. I hear sobs in her speech. I close my eyes. I wish I could put my hands under the door, so she knew I was there. My voice has to be enough for now.

'Do you wanna talk about it?'

'Can you just stay here?'

'Sure.' We sit together with the door dividing us, for a while. I listen to my heartbeat, count the spaces between.

'Last night was rough,' she says. I nod. I imagine most nights are somehow – rough customers, rushing around, drunken young idiots who feel like sober brave men – but this one must've been more.

'It's alright. You're through it.'

'I...I...' she starts to say, but stops. I exhale, sharply, and look out of the window. The sun shines, though I still see a few raindrops on the glass. The sun dances light through the drops like kaleidoscopes.

'If you open the door,' I say, 'I'll make breakfast. Yeah?'

Silence. Moments stretching into something longer than a lifetime. I hear movement, and stand up. A key turns in the lock, and for a moment *I think of the sound an M16A2 makes when you reassemble the charging handle back into the main body during maintenance.* A wistful click.

A PLACE TO BURY HORSES

Christy opens the door, and stands to the side, so I can't see her.

'Come, come in,' she says. The words sound like they hurt her. I see packets of cigarettes on the table, some empty. Her ashtray is a graveyard. She closes the door behind me, and I see she's wearing a gray t-shirt, and pyjama shorts. Her legs and arms are bruised, some so badly I can see fingerprints. I don't think for a moment. Everything leaves me. She tucks her hair behind her ear again, and I see she's been crying all night. You can tell by a person's eyes. Like they have ghosts behind them. Alice had that look too, once.

'I...' she says. She puts her head in her hands, sobs once, and then falls to the ground, against the wall again. I step forward. Try and catch her. Miss. I stand for a moment, before crouching down in front of her. She reaches her arms out for me, and I hold her for a moment. The feeling of wanting to hurt the world boils into my heart. Everything feels of blackened burnt glass. Everything shatters. Even hearts.

A while later, she's calmer. I make her breakfast while she showers. I make eggs, use some salmon I found. Alice used to joke I was a great cook – I think I was, once. I make her coffee, and I sit by the window in a wicker chair, her on the couch. She takes a cigarette with shaky hands. I look into her eyes as she speaks, and I see a little life in them. I worry, though, that finally something has taken that big wild heart she has away.

'This guy at work. My boss. Tony, he, you know, he's a business man. He likes to, to make sure...people, are, you know, happy. I can't...I can't do this again.'

'Right.'

'So, I...he, I mean, I used to...' She looks at the table, brow furrowed.

'I used to live around here, worked at the Pearl before. When this guy called Weeks owned it. He, um, he died. I don't know. He was old, I guess,' she looks at the ceiling. I see bruises around her throat, light ones. Second pressure on my trigger finger. My hand spasms and I have to put it in my jacket pocket to hide it till the storm of electricity in the muscle there is still.

'I moved away, for a while, you know, wanted to go to Portland. I, um...I, I didn't have any money, so I moved back here. I'm, I'm saving up enough to go home, maybe live at the ranch again.'

Her shoulders slump. Gave all of herself into the admission. I nod. I understand.

'I just, you know.' She shakes her head, closes her eyes. She puts down the coffee, and takes a long painful drag of the cigarette. It's enough to make me wince. I don't, and instead I look out of the window to the street below. I think of sovereignty, an old world word. It means someone in complete control and authority. I wonder how many people have either thing. I wonder how many deserve it.

'I'm sorry,' she says, and I turn, trying to smile and not managing it. She notices that but ignores it. I think the sentiment counts. I don't know how I feel. I hear laughter outside. A family were walking down the street, a small girl with a man and woman. All were holding hands. I look at Christy. A few loose tears fall down her face, but she wipes them away. They are just residual things.

'Christy,' I say. She turns to me, quick gulps of breath in shudders. 'Do you want to go somewhere?'

*

A while later, and we're sat in silence in the car. I text Bones on the way – tell him I'm heading to the ranch, and if he could be so kind, to make room for us. He doesn't reply with anything other than "okay." She doesn't know where we're going. I remember what she said when we first spoke – she mentions a ranch, no doubt a ranch where she was from. Bones has a small ranch just off the track by the gun range. Guess he wants his horses nearby. Maybe they give him comfort with the late hours. I don't know.

Christy doesn't say anything. She sits as a statue, staring out of the window. Her arms. They are strewn with bruises like cracks in the brickwork of a decayed house. I want to reach out. Don't. Instead

I put the radio on. Betty Lake, again. Best damn radio station in Oregon.

'...joy to us all. That's what we all want, right? This is the part of the show where I take in calls from you, lovely Oregonians...man, what a fun word that is...and we talk for a time. Us all, let's share that together, huh?'

'I'm sorry,' Christy says. She still faces the window. She closes her eyes; I can see that in the reflection. I smile at her though she can't see me.

'You haven't done anything wrong. I promise, okay?'

'I don't know,' she says. She turns away from the window, looks straight ahead as trees bleed past. 'Where are we going?'

'We're nearly there. I think you need it.' We drive past the range, the occasional light pop of something I recognise as a Glock. The occasional air shredding burst of semi-automatic fire. I even hear the M1 Garand again. The noise is loud, true. A scream from nearly a century ago. I hear it all the way till we reach the edge of forest that marks the boundary to his ranch. Christy looked around at the farmhouse in the distance, the barn. She looked outside of her window to where the horses were; the sun carving them out. Shadows. They look like roaming shadows. I see a smile creep onto her face.

'Feeling better already?'

A PLACE TO BURY HORSES

She doesn't say anything. She watches the horses roam around. I smile. Bones is stood there on the porch, Marybeth stood next to him. She used to be a stripper, sure; the years hadn't been kind to her, though. I think Bones would agree. I don't know. She has a quiet kindness though – the kind only a mother could have. She wasn't one, but she had the feelings for it. So it boded well – it meant that she was genuinely a good person.

Bones is stood there in a faded Metallica t-shirt, blue jeans, and large brown cowboy boots. His beard shakes in a warm breeze. His smile is just as warm. He waves at me, stepping down off the porch, whilst Marybeth waves and smiles from her perch. I pull over onto the gravel, and step out. Christy is all smiles. She looks over at the horses in the corral. Watches them as they trot. A young pony hugs the flank of its mother. She raises her tattooed hand to her mouth for a moment, involuntarily. It's like I've took her home, if only for one day.

'Ah, Joel!'

'Bones,' I say. I look at his wife. 'Marybeth.'

'Joel,' she says. She looks at Christy. 'And who might this little lady be?'

'Christy,' Christy says. She tucks her hair behind her ears. 'Um, Christy. Sorry. I.. Is this your place?'

'Yes it is, Miss Christy,' Bones says. He shakes my hand. 'Marybeth is feeding them later, if ya'll want to join?'

'I'd...yes.' Christy looks at me, her eyes finally showing some of that big heart I knew she had. She looks at me with eyes that say thank you. I nod at her like she'd said it. Marybeth shakes Christy's hand, and then looks to me.

'You two staying for dinner?'

'If that's okay,' I say. Bones smiles, pats me on the back. Christy looks all round the ranch. Memories flood in, a levee broken. The forest shields us from the outside. A world of something more lies just past them. We don't need it.

Dinner is fine; something traditional. Fried chicken and mash potatoes. Bones is as far from the man he used to be I'd ever seen. He used to ride loud machines along the bones of highways with dangerous men. Now he owned a ranch and ran a gun range. His wife used to be a stripper, who stopped when she found out she preferred tending to the farm over writhing around a pole. Neither looks like what they used to be; at least not all the way. I think Marybeth trained to be a nurse once. The world didn't want her that way. Made her something else.

The conversation is, admittedly, delightful. There's an ease to talking in there. Even I laugh.

'So, that was how we met,' Bones says, finishing a story I've heard a dozen times. Christy is enraptured. Maybe she didn't know there was a world like what Bones had described. Marybeth blushes.

'So he just, he just jumped into your car?'

'Yeah. He's there, buckshot all up his side, and I recognise him as the biker who stood up for me at work,' Marybeth says. She looks at Bones like a princess regarding a wayward but well meaning knight.

'How did, how would you even get away from something like that, that life?' Christy asks. I think she means more than a simple question. I think this is something of importance for her. Marybeth passes the plate of chicken to Bones, who passes it to me.

'Sometimes if you know something is worth it, you find ways to leave the old things behind.' I nod. Wisdom in that.

Later, the sun begins to set and Marybeth and Christy are stood by the corral. Horses are coming up to them, and they're being fed by hand. Christy waves at me. I wave back. Me and Bones are stood on the porch, smoking. His cigarettes taste of soot and crushed leaves. I swear I feel the grit of sand.

'She seems nice,' Bones says. I nod. Don't say anything else. Bones does instead. 'You know, me and Marybeth have a lot of distance, age wise, a good fifteen years, even, and...'

A PLACE TO BURY HORSES

'Don't go there,' I say. Bones smiles, before snorting a laugh out.

'Just saying, man. I worry about you. You come to the range a lot, and, you know, we talk and the like. Just worried is all.'

'Yeah,' I say. I watch as Christy gently strokes the snout of a horse, from between its eyes to the nose. Marybeth laughs loudly at something Christy says. I smile as I speak.

'I need to buy a gun,' I say.

'Um, what?' Bones says. He laughs. Thinks I'm joking. My expression gives away I'm not.

'I want to buy the 1911 I fired the other day. I just, you know. I'm a soldier, you know? We like our firearms. Especially ones as old as that.'

'I don't know,' Bones says. He looks at the ground, spits just off his porch. He looks up at the setting sun. His tattoos are faded on his arms, but I make out spiders on them.

'I don't think that's a good idea, um, I just...I just don't. I was just, you know, um, thinking you were alone, and, and you...'

'I'm not going to shoot myself,' I say. I say it bluntly, and I see Bones close his eyes. He shakes his head. The brusqueness must've stung.

'I...I didn't, I, I didn't mean that...'

'I know,' I say. I don't, though. That was what he thought, clearly. I watch the sun set. Bones is silent for a time. I watch Christy feed more horses. She's happy for the first time all day. I smile.

'I don't even, like...it was from a gun show, man, no papers.'

'Is that a problem?'

'No, but...Joel, you're my friend and all, but you know.'

'I'll give you three thousand dollars,' I say. I mean it, too.

'I...what do you even want it for anyway? The thing is old, it'll need maintenance, and it might not be one hundred percent reliable...'

'That might be why I want it,' I say. Christy and Marybeth make their way back up the hill to the farm house. Christy is beaming. I smirk, and turn to Bones. I place a hand on his shoulder – like we're friends.

'I just think I'd feel safer with it, is all.' Liv has a black eye. She tries to blame it on herself.

'I...' Bones smirks. Shakes his head, closes his eyes. He sticks his hand out and I shake it. 'Alright, man. Alright. Sure. Can you come by the range tomorrow? I'll sort it out then.'

'Sure. I got work three till ten, then I'll, uh... I'll swing by beforehand.'

'Awesome. Alright,' he says. Marybeth laughs again at something Christy says, and smiles at me. Bones calls to his wife as a gentle breeze turns cool.

'Hey, now. What are ya'll laughing about?'

'Nothing,' Marybeth says. She hugs her husband, kisses his cheek. She heads inside, and Christy stands next to me, her hands in her pockets. I smile at her.

'Have fun?'

'I...yeah. I loved it.' She takes a glance at the corral. 'It was like being home.'

'Good,' I say. I turn to Bones. 'Well, we gotta get. Thanks for today, Bones. I'll see you tomorrow?'

'Sure, man. Miss Christy, a pleasure,' he says. He asks for her hand with his and he kisses it once, gently, on the back. She laughs.

*

The drive back is filled with warmth and silence. The deep, dark kind only found in the woods. The radio isn't on. There is the golden hue of the sun as it dies and sinks into the land. It's swallowed up by America.

'I loved today,' Christy says. She smiles and looks dreamily out of the window. 'Thank you,' she says. I nod. In my head, I already have the 1911 and it rests in a lockbox under my bed. It was a spur of the moment thing, to ask for it – but some part of me thinks it was anything but that. Something that I needed to make happen.

'Don't mention it,' I say, a thousand miles away. She turns to me, and rests her head back. She smiles at me warmly.

'So,' I say. I feel uncomfortable, the way she looks at me for only a heartbeat. It's too much. I feel something in my chest grow heavy. I count to four in my head, feel my breathing slow. 'What was it like on the ranch?'

She smiles shyly and turns away again. Looks out into the trees as the dying of the light creates beams of flame between their branches.

'It was great. It was a lot like what Bones has. You know, um, we were more of a...I guess, a traditional ranch, you know. Break in horses, um, you know. Sell them, and the like.'

'I get you,' I say as we reach Pine Oaks. The town sits at the base of the hill. 'Best memory there?'

'I'd have to think about that. I have so many, you know?'

'Yeah.'

'Can we go to the pier again, later?'

'Sure. Um. Sure.'

'Cool. Um, call for me in about an hour, we'll, um, you know.'

She says nothing more the whole drive back. Neither do I. I think about Liv. The way her face looked. I keep it to myself how I feel. Feels like a shadow rests itself over my heart. Something dark and long. I smile all the same to Christy. We walk together upstairs, passing Jay sat on the curb outside. I don't say anything to him. He doesn't say anything to me. Christy, neither. I walk with Christy along the hallway to our apartments, and she smiles as we reach our doors.

'An hour, okay?'

'Sure,' I say, as I turn to leave. As I do so, she gently takes my arm, holds me there. I'm stood, awkwardly, sideways. She takes a step forward and kisses my cheek, before letting go and going into her room. I stand for a moment, whilst the purple neon bleeds under her door. I don't know how to feel. Don't know what I've done – though I'm scared all the same. I go into my room and sit down, for a long, long moment. I don't even realize my answer phone is winking at me with a sharp red gaze. I stand up, feeling uneasy, and press play on the message.

'Hey, Joel, it's Gerald's son,' the machine says. I stand still for a moment, thinking.

'Um,' the machine continued, 'my dad, he, uh...he's sick. Up at Providence in Portland. Um...could, could you come and see him?

I know me and you don't really talk, and, you know...he, he just wants to see you. Thanks, Joel. Um. Just, you know. I'll leave you my number.' He did.

'Bye,' the machine says, as the message ends. I stand still. Doesn't make sense. I try to – but my brain doesn't work. I sit back on the chair in front of the TV, and simply stare at the screen. Nothing makes any sense. Nothing.

I send a text to Liv.

'Hey, it's Joel. I'm sorry for last night. Just don't like you being hurt.' I send it, but don't get a reply. I go over to the window, watch the sun finally die and disappear behind Mt Bachelor. I look at my watch. An hour has gone. I walk to Christy's room, but have no idea what I'm feeling. I can't put a finger on it. Something illusory. I knock on Christy's door, and she's wearing a pink and black striped dress, makeup. She's even put some on the bruises, and I feel even more uneasy about that. She smiles at me warmly, the black piercing through her nose catching the light. She picks up a cardigan looking thing of heavy grey knitting, and steps out of her apartment. She smells of summer flowers.

'Big guy,' she says, as she hugs me. I hug her back, tentatively. Something is wrong with me. A pit in my stomach. She kisses my cheek again. For a dangerous second I want to kiss her. Beat it back. Don't. She has a life still. 'So, pier and pizza?'

'Sure,' I say. We walk, for a time, back down through Pine Oaks to the inland pier. She links an arm with me, and speaks quietly.

'I, I'm sorry if I'm being a little, um, you know. Clingy,' she says. She turns away as we pass a DVD store. I look straight ahead. Trees create dark shadows at my peripheral. They're tall, so I see them over the roofs of buildings.

'I don't think you are. Don't worry.'

'Good,' she says. She nods once and repeats herself as she does so. 'Good.'

She shivers once in the cold, and we pass her friend, Olive, stood outside with a few other people. Girls Christy must work with. Some look too young. They're stood outside of a bar. A couple are a little drunk, most are sober and trying to keep up. Christy waves, smiles. They ask her if she's going for drinks, calling across the street. Christy calls back she'll text her. Olive wolf whistles. I realize she's drunk, too.

'Oh my God, I'm sorry,' Christy says. I smile.

'It's, uh, good. You should go out with your friends. They're all we have sometimes.' Christy looks at the floor, smiles.

'Would that be okay?'

A PLACE TO BURY HORSES

'You do what you want, little lady,' I say to her. She squeezes my arm tighter with a laugh. We reach the pier.

There is a certain curious moon above us that cuts down to the earth with bone-hued light. The water around us is dark. A void. Christy lights a cigarette, and we walk along the pier to the end. I light my own when we reach the end.

She stands close next to me, closer than she ever has done. We both look up at the moon. There are no boats around. No floating lights disappearing into the distance to destinations unknown. Just us two.

'Thank you again for today,' she says. I smile, nod.

'It's, fine. It's fine. I'm glad it...it helped, right?'

'Yeah. I like Mr and Mrs Rueman. They're um...characters.'

I laugh.

'Yeah, they are. They've done really, really good for themselves.'

'Yeah.'

A gentle breeze nuzzles up to us and the waves lap in the dark below us. You can hear it, if you listen. Christy rests her head on my shoulder. Only for a moment. The two of us stand there, smoking.

'A quiet moment,' I say. I don't know why I remember the saying, but I do. Christy lifts her head up, and looks up at me.

'What?'

'"A quiet moment, between the dreary ones." It's a saying, um. Like everyone gets a quiet moment with someone else that you don't share with anyone quite the same again,' I say. Christy nods. She stands on her tiptoes and kisses my cheek again. It's made somewhat warmer, because of the cold. I close my eyes. Part of me can feel her heartbeat, she's stood so close. I find comfort in the rhythm. She speaks to me quietly, as I feel her arm move away from mine. She looks up at me.

'I thought about what you said, earlier. I, um, I miss my horses', she says, smoking a cigarette. I see something human in the way her lips begin to curl, something loving, and she smiles at me warmly. She turns back towards the lake, which led out into the distance to the ocean. 'They're such innocent things. It's, uh, it's dumb, I mean...I'm....you know, what I am. I just kinda wish I'd...I...I wish I still had the farm, you know.'

'What was your favourite horse called?'

She stares out smiling. No answers for a moment, the silence a deep valley in the night, dangerous to fall into. She reaches over with her free hand, the tattooed one of beautiful flowers and her long black nails. Her hand rests on top of mine, and our fingers intertwine. She strokes my hand soothingly with her thumb. I don't see the stripper who lives next door anymore. I see a young girl, someone beautiful, with a whole heart to give yet still. I was wrong, earlier. She still could make it.

'Rose,' she says, not turning. 'My favourite one was called Rose.' I look down at her, and kiss the top of her head. Don't know why. We stand there, then, in silence, holding hands.

It's the perfect kind of quiet moment, and I wish it would last forever.

It doesn't.

*

Later, we're walking back to the bar where Olive and the others were. We hold hands still, and I feel something akin to calm. It's something deeper, though – like staring into a deep blue ocean. That feeling, in your heart. It's that. Christy is telling me about how she got the rose tattoos for her favourite horse.

'We buried her in a beautiful patch of forest on the land. It was hard, because she was my best friend, but...the place we, um, put her, it's beautiful.' I nod, smile. It's dangerous business to bury horses on the property – especially if they were euthanized with drugs, similar stuff. I agreed with Christy, though. They're not just animals. They're a part of you. Family.

She squeezes my hand for a second, a quick thing. I do the same back. Don't know what I'm doing. Suddenly her phone rings, loudly, and I recognize it as the band we heard on the radio, *Cromarty High.* She places it to her ear, a small careful smile on her face.

'Hey, Olive,' she says. She looks at me with a mock exasperated expression. 'Yeah, I'm on the way. No, Joel's, um...' Christy looks at me.

'Are you coming?' She whispers.

'Nah, I, uh. Work tomorrow. I'll, um, rain check.'

Christy smiles, and raises my hand to her mouth and kisses it once. I start to feel uncomfortable again, then. Something wasn't right.

'Joel's not coming,' Christy says. I hear Olive talking on the other end of the line. 'Yeah, I uh. Yeah. I'll tell you when I'm...Olive, uh. Yeah. I'll explain. No. Yeah. Olive, he doesn't...no. No. I'll talk to you soon, okay? '

I notice a tone there. Something I don't recognize the intent of.

'Alright, see ya soon!' Christy says as she hangs up. She looks up at me, and I see her smile in that tender way again. We reach the corner where the bar was. I see Christy look down at the floor.

'Can we, um, get pizza another time?'

'Sure. You know where I am,' I say. We cross the street and she looks up at me. She wraps her arms around my neck, and stands on her tiptoes again.

'Well, I'll see ya later, big guy,' she says.

'Little lady,' I say back. She kisses me on the lips, then. That feeling of unease. It's a voracious gnaw. Something dark, and cold. It twists my stomach into knots. I feel my heart race. She tastes of cigarettes and cherries. I feel my hands shake on her waist. I pull away.

'I, uh. I'll see ya later, yeah?' I say to her as I turn away. The world is moving fast. Panic attack. That was it. I close my eyes. I couldn't do with breaking her heart.

'I, uh, yeah! Rain-check!' she says. I smile, though my mind's starting to slip and the world is going ugly.

'Call for me!' she says.

I feel like I should say something. Maybe I should stay – there is something in my mind that speaks in a concave scream. There is a warning written in the night, like I'd heard something or seen something dangerous.

We'd leave, go to Portland. Texas. Anywhere she wants.

Anywhere other than where we are.

*

STYX LANE GUNRANGE, OREGON
10:30 AM

I arrive early for the gun, and the sun shines brightly down on me in approval. Styx Lane is quiet. I hear no gunfire as I approach. I step out of my car, breathe in fresh air. Force it from my lungs.

Bones is stood outside, smoking. He's shaved his beard off. He waves at me as he sees me leave the car and walk up the gravel, towards the store. He stamps the cigarette down into the earth.

'Joel, hey man!'

'Bones,' I say. We shake hands. He looks younger now, without the beard. His face seems gentler – he overall seems gentler. I don't say anything about it. Bones pats me on the back, and we walk into the range talking for a time.

'So, how was your night?'

'I went home. Took Christy out to the pier for a while.'

'Oh, the romance.'

'Shut up,' I say. Bones laughs.

We decide to shoot for a time. I practice with the 1911. I notice that the rear sight doesn't quite match up with the foresight. I have to compensate somewhat for that. It's a little wide. It could be a problem, if I ever decide to shoot at something moving. I pause for a moment at that. Don't know where the thought comes from. I'm staring at the slide of the pistol, pulled back to expose an empty chamber. The thought still remains. Bones stands looking at me, reeling in the target. Sees me, staring at the pistol like it had fallen off the moon.

'You, uh, okay there?' He asks. I look at him, my thoughts broken. What was I thinking? Probably about beautiful people getting hurt all the time. By men like me. I look at him, picking up a new magazine from the table next to me.

'I'm, uh. I'm fine,' I say. Part of me wishes that the part saying it was a lie would shut up.

'Good. You're seeming a little off, today. If it was the thing I said about Christy, I'm, you know, sorry.'

'Nah, ain't that.' The target reels in, and I see two of the seven rounds fired were wide of center mass. Bones wipes off the powdery residue, and places the target on the box. He looks at it, before looking back at me.

'Damn thing can't shoot straight, huh?'

'No.' I was referring to me. Not just with firearms.

Later, we're in his office, a place that no doubt was left over from the biker bar era. A deer head rests on the wall, the eyes haunting. A Harley engine sits on the wall above Bones, held by large metal spikes. A mural of a biker woman is on the wall behind. I see parts where it has faded – Bones' tried to get rid of it, before changing his mind. An old bleeding heart.

'So, um, we good for the cash you told me yesterday? Three?'

'Yeah,' I say. I bring out the envelope of money I took out of my savings account at the bank. I know I have the money. I wasn't left penniless after the forces. This was a large chunk of it however. An irreparable amount. Bones uses an old letter opener knife. I see it has the Texan flag on it. I remember, idly while he counts the money, the flag of America my father had hung on a wall till one day he took it down. Never said why or where it went. I went to bed, and woke up to find it gone.

'And...yeah. Yeah, we're good.' Bones smiles at me, and places the envelope on the desk. He smiles at me. There's something in his eyes, though.

'Joel, I'm going to be one hundred percent on the level here, bro. You aren't thinking of something stupid are you?'

I eject the magazine, and pull back the slide. The one in the chamber flies out, lands on the table. Rolls for a time, skittish like a deer on ice, before settling. I place the mag on the table, and take a seat across from Bones on one of the plastic chairs he always brings out when I shoot at night.

'No, Bones. I'm fine. I need to ask, though – you got any spare mags? And possibly a holster?'

'I'll...I'll have a look. Mags, I know. Holster, um, I might have something ugly I can throw at you.'

'Sure.'

'Need .45's too?'

'Yeah. Just a box.'

'Who the fuck are you going to war with?' Bones asks. There's an incredulous expression on his face. I shrug. Don't know myself.

'Joel, if you're, like, in trouble, or, or...' he says, folding his arms. When he looks at me now, I see there is something old within his eyes. Some tethered rage in his heart. Marybeth had helped him bury it.

I see it, there. Just underneath. She would help him, to tie the old ghosts within him to the leaden coffins of time. But they were always there. Reminders of who you are. Just underneath.

'I...I know how things can be. Just sometimes. I know how things can be.'

'Bones. I'm fine. Sort me a holster and a couple spare mags, a box of .45. We're all good. I'm all good.'

Bones doesn't believe me. He does believe, though, that I've given him three thousand dollars for a gun that can't be traced. No papers. Gun show. Like he said. I don't know if that's what he thinks. It's what I'd think, though.

'Joel...okay. You have to, *have* to let me know, though, that you're okay.'

'I'm fine,' I say. Reach forward; put the bullet back into the magazine. Fit the magazine into the pistol grip. Don't lift a round. Leave the safety on. It sits on the table in front of me.

'I'm fine,' I say.

*

I call in sick again, after. I drive for a time, just around. I go through the woods, through open plains and forests. I just drive. I think I'm halfway to Warm Springs when I pull over at the side of the road. I see a horse in a field, on its own. It stands silhouetted by the sun. It looks at me, then around. Then at the sun. I stand by the fence, a dilapidated wooden thing that smells like a forest in the rain. The 1911 is in the car. I smoke, and look at the horse. I reach for my phone, and call Alice. It's a number I don't think about calling. Don't even know if it's hers anymore. I do it through memory. Don't know why.

'Hello, Alice Denver speaking.'

'Alice,' I say. There's a pause of static. Something cold. I look at the horse as it feeds on the ground before pacing.

'Joel? Jesus.'

'I, I know. I'm sorry. I, I kinda just. Um.'

'Joel, I can't...I'm in work. Are you okay?'

'I...I just wanted to see how you were.'

'Joel, are you okay?'

'Yeah. I'm fine.'

'Joel, okay, listen. I, I don't know, what you're, you're thinking, calling me...but, but if it's to say sorry, then, you don't, don't have to. Wyatt, that wasn't your fault.'

I close my eyes. She could never hide a lie to me. They are always as clear and as cold as crystal, no matter how she said them.

'We both know it was.'

'Joel, it wasn't. You need to...are you, are you drunk?'

'Yes,' I lie. 'I'm sorry.'

'Joel...look, um, call me when you're sober, okay?'

'Will do,' I say. I hang up. I close my eyes. Realize where I was driving to. Didn't think. I get back in the car, heading up to Crooks Hollow penitentiary. It's near enough the other side of

Oregon, between Unity and Vale on the 26. It takes me a couple hours. I realize I haven't been to Crooks Hollow in years. *Not since a rainy night with Wyatt in a car, after a Halloween carnival.*

The place reeks of ghosts.

*

I get scanned at the entrance, after looking online for when the visiting hours were. Three till four. I make it with half an hour to kill. I think, then, about what I wanted the pistol for. As I sit there, just outside the gates in the car, I think about storms. About being perfectly, irreparably dangerous, if just for a heartbeat. I think about storms.

I leave the pistol in the car, for the sake of better judgement.

'Name of prisoner?'

'Ray Corfey.'

'Sure. Sign the register.' I do. No point lying. I get lead through to the visiting room. It's almost like what I imagine it to be. Seats in front of a glass wall, dividers between the seats so as to separate everyone. A phone on a cord, built into the wall. A notice on the wall says "All calls may be recorded for monitoring and security." I nod. Don't know if there's truth to that. Don't much care.

Ray sits on the other side. Down at the further cubicle. A guard escorts me down, before making his way back up to the door.

Ray looks at me for a moment. Doesn't recognize me. I see it dawn on him. See the recognition flare in his eyes like a tempest of fire. I sit down. He looks at me for a moment. His grey eyes. He's lost weight. Lost hair. Still wears glasses, though. I take the phone from the wall. He does the same. I see his hands shake, only slightly. A tremor.

'Hi.'

'I...what are you doing here?'

'Thought I'd see you.'

A pause. I think of him. *I think of him stood on the banking of a hill, calling the police. His car is parked, the front dented. Rain. He's drunk, crying. He keeps saying sorry. Rain.*

'What do...I...I'm sorry,' he says. A few tears stain the inside of his glasses. 'I, I don't, I'm sorry. I don't drink anymore.'

'I know. I know a few things. I know you get out in three years, eight months and six days, on parole. Marked it on a calendar.'

'I...oh, God, mister, I'm, I...I didn't think right, I, I...'

'I know. I have been, though. Been thinking about you. Thinking right.' He sobs, once.

'Shut the fuck up,' I say. He sniffles, once. Looks at me. His gray eyes, framed in bloodshot white.

A PLACE TO BURY HORSES

Rain.

Shake the thought from my head. I look at him, for a moment, feel something like pity. My hand still feels recoil from the 1911. Feel it in the bones, there.

'I just want you to know that. I've been thinking about you a lot. About me. What happened. Things like time. Fecundity. I've been thinking about how you get out soon. I want you to know that.' I hang up. Leave. Ray sits there, silent.

I go into my car, visitors' lot, and wrap my fists around the steering wheel. I look at the healing bruises on my hand from when I punched the wall. Feels a lifetime ago. Only a few days.

I left, heading back home. The whole time there I'm shaking from adrenaline. Can't think.

Can't think at all. Spend a couple days like that. Can't think. *Rain.*

*

PART THREE:

NOTHING TO BE

PINE OAKS, OREGON
9:00AM

I sit in my apartment for a time, a few days later. I haven't written anything in a while – forgot. I'll do some later. A while later. Not now. I've told Liz I've had to go out of town a few days. I look out of the window to Pine Oaks, see the main street. Quiet. Nothing to do, nothing to see. No one to meet, nothing to be. I look at the sun. It's a monolithian thing older than everything. I wonder who put it there sometimes.

My phone rings. Christy. Still don't know what to think. She shouldn't have kissed me – I knew that. She had a big, beautiful heart. I doubted I even had one. I let my phone ring a little. Think about it.

Then I remember the way she had been with the horses, remembering when life was simple, clean, and I pick up.

'Hey, big guy,' she says. She's a little breathless – her voice is croaky. Probably smoked some weed she couldn't handle. I look out of the window. The sky is all ocean.

'Hey little lady,' I say. There's a pause, for a moment. I hear her breathing erratically. For a moment, I think she's crying.

'Hey, are you alright?'

'I...I. Yeah. I, yeah. I'm fine. Just, you know. Hung-over. Little cold. Um... Can you come over? Or, or I go over to you?'

'I...sure. I mean, you can just talk to me through the walls, but yeah. Give me ten minutes and I'll come over.'

'I...thanks. Thank you, Big Guy,' she says. I catch her shuddering a breath out as the line clicks to static. I think for a moment, before throwing on clothes and heading out. I leave the pistol in a kitchen drawer. I knock on her door, and she answers. Wearing an oversized black t-shirt, *Re-Animator* starring Jeffrey Combs. Shorts, knee highs.

She knuckles sleep from her eyes. Makeup still on. I suppose it was the passed out option, then. I go in, and see there are even more dead cigarettes in the ashtray. Some spill onto the coffee table. I wonder if she's slept, and if she has, how soundly. I surmise not too well.

'Hey,' I say, as she closes the door behind me. She hugs me from behind, and I feel her shake. Something happened. I turn around, and she wraps her arms around my neck. Her hair is in her face, and she looks down. I pull her close.

'What's wrong?'

'I...oh God...' She says. Buries her face in my chest. I feel her heartbeat. Fast. Panic. That singular kind you feel in the pit of your stomach, the bottom of your heart. She shudders once, before taking a deep breath. I don't know what to do.

'Sorry,' she says. 'I'm sorry.'

'Hey,' I say. We walk over to the couch. She sits down, and I sit on the table, facing her. I light a cigarette, offer her one. She shakes like there's ice in her bones, but she manages it. I light it for her.

'Real, real classy,' she says, laughing a little through tears. She wipes her eyes with the back of her hand. Her makeup runs.

'I try,' I say with a shrug. I don't want the night we kissed to come up. I think mistakes were made. Mine was being me, hers for having that kind of love to give to me.

'I...I'm sorry. I –' her phone rings, on the table next to me. She lets it ring, and the sound of *Cromarty High* cuts off after the chorus to *Amy*. I look at her.

'Are you okay?'

'I...yeah, Big Guy, now you're here. I, I had an argument with Olive last night...'

'Oh. I'm sorry. You guys are, uh, good friends...'

'Yeah –' Her phone interrupts her. Rings again. She looks at it on the table next to me like a ghost is calling her. It's a quick glance, one I catch. It goes dead again. She looks at me, trying not to show anything.

'Olive keeps, um, calling me. You know, trying to, to be, um...'

'Christy, what's happened?'

'I...' she looks down for a moment, then through me. Her gaze is one I've seen before. The kind that belies horrors. Something had happened to her, the night I left. If I'd know. Only if I'd know, God, I wouldn't have gone. I didn't know. Didn't.

'I'm okay,' she says. Her gaze focuses again. The world grows structure to it. She pulls herself back from a memory. 'You wanna go for breakfast? I need, like, thirty waffles.'

'I...sure.'

We go to a waffle place off the main street, near West Street. We don't talk about the phone. We just talk. With pauses, feelings. It isn't until the walk back that Christy asks me something. We don't hold hands, don't kiss. Something like a sheet of glass between us.

'Joel...in, um. In the army. Did you...um...'

'Did I...?'

'Okay. I, I don't think it's cool for me to ask.'

'It's fine,' I say. I don't know if it is. Don't know. Any soldier knows the questions civilians ask. They don't mean to – but they do.

'I, well. You, uh...you must've, um, seen, you know. Things.'

'I did.' Don't think. Don't.

'So, uh...did, does it, get, easier?'

'After a time. For a while, it's...it's hard to explain.' A feeling in my chest. It's like fear, but it swallows you up in panic. I heard a friend of mine once couldn't sleep in a bed for a month while on leave between tours. He slept on the floor with a backpack under his head. It reminded him of his pack, I guess. I wonder if the night reminded him of the desert.

'I'm sorry,' she says. I reach for her hand, hold it. Her fingers wrap around mine again, but I feel hesitance.

'It's okay,' I say. Christy looks at me with a delicate, curious smile. I can't explain what it conveyed. Something deeper than understanding, maybe. She stops at a halt, and kisses me. I don't know what to think, other than something had happened to her. She pulls herself close to me. She closes her eyes after the kiss, smiles to herself.

'I'm stood on my tip-toes,' she says with a breathy laugh. I smile at her.

'You got work today?' I ask.

'I, um...I don't know. Maybe. I'll see. Why?'

'Wondered if you wanted to –'

Her phone rings. She looks at the screen, as *Cromarty High* sings about having outstretched arms.

'I...um, give me a second,' she says. She kisses me again, let's go of my hand. Walks a few feet away, a finger to her other ear. I light up a cigarette, look in a bookstore window. *Years of The Worm,* by Robert Hull. Never read it. Heard it was Stephen King-Lite, which holds no appeal. I don't need any more horror.

Christy comes back, and smiles. She's shaken, though. The call.

'I, um, I have work tonight. Um, could, do you want to go back to mine? We, um, can...I have wine?' She says. Her tone implies a question, and I smile. Look at my watch.

'It's like, 11AM.'

'Yeah, I know,' she says. Takes my hand. 'We have catching up to do!'

I laugh, smile. I think about the phone, of course. The calls in the apartment, just now. I figure she'll tell me, when it's time. When she's ready. If there is anything to tell.

These lies we tell ourselves.

There's never, really, ever time when we need it. It slips away. Never have the right time.

*

Christy and I sit on the couch. Drunk by 1PM. It's fine, though – there's an ease to the conversation after a few glasses. The wine is horrible, but we talk through it. I'm thinking about writing more of the book, later, when Christy comes in. She's wearing the things again from earlier, minus the knee high socks. She carries the two glasses of wine with difficulty. I see her giggle under her breath, as she passes me the glass. I don't take it immediately, lost in thoughts about the story.

'Hello?' She asks, and I shake my head and take the glass. She sits next to me on the couch, the TV showing some movie from a long time ago that Christy loves. There's something of a quiet to Christy after drinking. I think about her sat outside her front door, wanting to apologize for the noise. My mind drifts.

'Where were you just now?' She asks. She sits so her legs are over me across my lap. I don't feel comfortable at all, but I don't say anything. It's what men do. Christy swills the drink around in the glass.

'I was thinkin' about my story.'

'Oh? What story? Also, when you drink wine your accent slips out.'

'I, ah, yeah. Yeah. It does, don't it? I'm sorta writin' somethin'.'

'Oh, you'll have to let me proof it. You know. Not just a pretty face,' she says with a laugh. She takes a sip of the wine. She's drinking a lot, I notice. I know drinking like that. It's the kind to burn something out of you. Like there was something to forget.

'Sure.'

She clumsily places the glass on the table, wine drops on the wood. The unease I've felt increases tenfold. It's the kind where you want to run. Outside, I see the sun. Christy gently places a hand on the back of my neck, and I turn to face her. Smile. Don't feel right.

The desert floods back. I try and smile. Slipping. Christy leans forward, and pulls me into a kiss. It's drunken. I feel my breath quicken. *Flashes of things in my mind. I see smoke on the plains of Afghanistan. An oil well. A man shredded in the front seat of a car, a dead pregnant woman in the back. The night, cool. Rain. Liv, with a black eye. I'm holding my friend behind a wall in a village, as the hole in his throat bleeds his life into the ground. I hold a woman I've never met, in the night in the desert, after a mine has destroyed the car the family drove in. She's crying to me in a language I don't understand. I think she's saying her daughter's name, but the little*

girl is in pieces. I try and comfort her whilst she dies. I don't know
what to do.

Christy straddles me, holding me close whilst she kisses me.

I feel rain on myself. Like I'm drowning. The windscreen. I
can just see out of it, through the blood on my face. Ray is stood on
the banking of the hill. I hear him swearing and crying into his
phone. Rain. My back. Don't think about it. Wyatt. He's what
matters. Get out of the car. Don't think. Don't.

I pick her up, and I carry her to the bedroom. Don't know
why. It's hard to focus. She's young. This isn't right, not at all. I kiss
her like I should, all the same.

I'm slamming the glass down at Rosie's. Liv is crying.

Christy is giggling whilst she takes her t-shirt off. She
reaches up and takes mine off. Pulls me in close, wrapping her legs
around my waist.

I sit with Alice in the dark. 'You hold me different,' I say.

Christy is looking up at me, her eyes wide. Concerned. I
don't realize I'm crying. My heart's beating fast. Things are still
flashing in my mind. A line of photographs. Like a reel of film. I
shake my head.

'Joel, what's...did I do something wrong?'

'No, I...' I stand up, wiping my eyes with the back of my hand. Stupid. I'm stupid.

'Joel,' she says. She covers herself with her arms. I realize my scars on my back are showing. The shame boils over into something more.

I'm trying to stand up in the rain. Ray is calling to me from the hill. I can't see. Everything is blurry. Feel blood on my back. Some of it isn't mine. I can tell by how it feels.

'I'm sorry,' I say. I go and get my t-shirt. Throw it on. Christy is crying on the bed. She looks at me like I'd done something irreparable. I think I have.

'Joel, wait, I, I'm sorry, I...'

'I know. I. I can't do this. I'm not right.'

'Joel, I don't...' She stands up, follows me to the living room. I throw my jacket on. She follows me. Speaks with slurred words.

'Joel, I don't need you right. You're a genuinely nice, you're a nice guy, and –'

'I killed my son,' I say. The silence is loud enough to shatter windows. Like an IED on a dusty road. I feel drunk, and angry. I need air.

To walk.

A PLACE TO BURY HORSES

To go anywhere.

I leave her in the living room.

*

PINE OAKS

Sometime later.

I sober up later, after passing out on my bed in my clothes. I check my phone – the screen's cracked. Don't remember doing it. Head feels like a war drum, filled with coals and stones. I think about Christy.

Stupid. I'm so fucking stupid.

I put my head in my hands. Can't remember what time it is, let alone the day. I stagger to my living room. I panic, for a brief time – I go to the kitchen, my heart racing, and check for the gun. Still in the drawer. However, I notice it's loaded now. I eject the magazine. Try and catch memories long since sunken. I can't pull them out. I look at the ceiling; feel something heavy in my chest like shame. I don't think it's all the way that – not all the way. I sink to my floor; lay with my back to the drawer. The pistol lies at my feet. I know the magazine isn't in – there's one in the chamber. I think about that, for a cold series of minutes that stray into an hour. I think about how everyday is the same.

I lift the pistol, gently, and press the barrel behind my right ear. That's the ideal point – where the nerves from the brain leak into your spine and then throughout the rest of your body like vines or the roots of trees. There's no coming back from that. I sit there, wide eyed. I keep my finger flat against the slide, not even in the trigger guard. I sit like that for a time. The feeling of being dangerous comes over me in a wave of icy fire. I place the pistol back down with shaking hands. I put my head into them in lieu. Can't think. Can't. I stand up. Christy. I need to, to do something. I stand, uneasy. Feel like my spine is made of glass. I throw a t-shirt on – I think the one I wore earlier – and stagger out of the door.

I knock on Christy's door; hear nothing on the other side but space. I take a step back, slide against the wall on the other side of the hallway. I close my eyes, before standing up and sliding against the door. I think of what to say. Can't.

'I...if you're there, I, I'm sorry. I...' I shake my head. 'I'm sorry you got me.' I stand up. I didn't know it, but I'd never really see her again. Not till they found her.

Even then, not really.

I decide to drive up to Portland, see Gerald. I think about everyone else on the drive there.

*

PORTLAND, OREGON
5:00 PM

I think I taste snow in the air as I reach Portland. It's a weird feeling of the cold in my mouth. It works in conjunction with the casually dead grey sky. It's like everything had begun to rot, that the sky was in the process of turning into a ghost itself. Some revenant of a healthy thing. I pull into the hospital car park and sit for a time. I look up at the encroaching clouds. I don't think about how myself and Alice used to live in the city. I close my eyes to remember for a moment.

We sit in on a bench in Washington Park. Feel something akin to warmth from inside myself. Something fleeting I knew in some quiet place I wouldn't get back. Alice kisses me gently on the cheek. We buy balloons. Let them go.

I light a cigarette in the car, staring at the windows of the hospital reception. A woman with red curly hair sits behind the desk, chewing a pencil. She looks at something on the desk in front of her, obscured from view. I close my eyes, breath dark fumes into the roof of the car. I tune into Betty Lake, listen to a song called *Candy Girl* by *Trailer Trash Tracys*. I hear it, but doesn't sink in. I wonder about Gerald in Vietnam. I wonder if he knew my pa.

A PLACE TO BURY HORSES

I get out of the car and crush the half finished cigarette under my boot. Walk into the reception. The redhead looks up. I see it's some kinda puzzle book, or a crossword.

'Hey,' she says, smiling. I smile back. In truth, all I'm thinking about is how the gun felt behind my ear. I don't know whether I could face fading away like Gerald might be. I don't know. 'How can I help?'

'I, uh, I'm looking for my friend. He was admitted, ah, a couple days ago.'

'Name hun?'

'Gerald Pryce.'

'Ah, let me have a little look.' She turns slightly to a computer, a slick thing that looks carved of alabaster and chrome. She scrolls with the mouse a couple times, while I look around the empty reception. Reminds me of a tomb of Perspex and disinfectant.

'I...here we are. Yep, Gerald Pryce. If you go over to the lift, uh, and head to Oncology, you'll find him in room 2B.'

'I...thanks.' As I walk to the lift the word settles in. *Oncology.* I stand in the lift, covered in mirrors that distort me just enough to hide me from myself. I know it's me, though. I close my eyes, bow my head. I'm not thinking of anything. Walking through dreams.

A PLACE TO BURY HORSES

I head to room 2B, and see Gerald there. He's lost weight. His face hangs off his skull loosely, a ghoul. His eyes still carry that twinkle, though – that thing that kept him alive in the jungle, kept him human. He smiles at me with a slightly open mouth, and I smile back. There are a few other people – maybe sicker than him, maybe not – but I ignore them.

'Well, if ain't you,' Gerald says. I nod, walk into the room. There's a seat right next to him, some comfortable looking thing of plastic and cushion. He lifts a hand up to me. I didn't notice at first, but clear tubing is held in his nose. I see a drip next to him. I feel something dark in my chest. I take his hand. He feels like tissue paper. How had it come so quickly? Maybe I hadn't noticed? I don't know. All I know, in this moment, is that Gerald is dying.

'Young man,' I say. He smiles, and I sit next to him. I furrow my brow as I take my seat. Gerald was still sharp.

'I, ah, well. You know.'

'How long have you known?'

'Fell over a few months ago. Came into hospital to get my hip looked at. Found a flurry of snow in my lungs.'

I shake my head; close my eyes for a second, before looking at him.

'Jesus, Gerald.'

'I know. I was a little surprised too.'

'You could've told me, you, you know that. You could've told me.'

'Yeah, that would've made our drinking and talking a lot more uplifting.'

'I...Gerald, fuck.' I close my eyes, look at him again. 'Fuck.'

He closes his eyes, and his smile falters for a second. Then comes back brighter.

'You know, it's funny. Kinda,' he says.

'How?'

'You're the one who smokes the shitty cigarettes. 50% glass, 40% sand.' He laughs.

'But I got the other 10% to be thankful for,' I say. I close my eyes, before smiling. He was still Gerald. He'd take that with him. We talk about his son, for a time – how he'd been supporting his dad this long. Gerald had nothing but praise for his son – never heard him speak like this before. He loved his boy. I wonder if my father loved me, too, at the end. I didn't know. I'd imagine he did, but just couldn't put it in words – least to me. Perhaps my Ma. Maybe he gave a little of his soul to his wife before the rest of it left him.

'Gerald,' I ask. The question from the parking lot burned in my head. 'Did you know my Pa? At all, like, in 'Nam?'

'I...yeah. I knew your Pa. He was in infantry, right? 3rd Platoon, ah, I forget the nickname, ah...'

'Yes.'

'Ah. You know, when you took that medal, I thought, "holy shit. It's John." Had to check the name twice. Joel, John. They're so damn similar.'

'How did you know him?'

'I saved his life, once. By association.'

'Huh.'

'It was a small war in a jungle.'

'It's a small world. It's all jungle still.'

'You wanna know what happened?'

'I...'

I think for a heartbeat or two, looking at the linoleum of the floor.

'No. Let's not. Let's leave the war behind.'

He smiles, before chuckling. His coughs come in a painful, fiery wave. He says he feels it in every space of his chest. Like someone left irradiated rocks in there. It didn't feel like snow.

'It's too damn hot,' he said. I smiled, a little worried. More than once I saw his teeth and the back of his hand flecked with tiny red drops. We talk. I pretend I don't notice, but he knows better than to call me out for being a bad liar. Eventually a male nurse comes in, blonde hair trendy and short.

'Hey, I'm really sorry, guys, but, um, visiting hours are nearly up.'

I look at my watch. 9:20PM. Visiting ends at half past. I nod at him, and he smiles.

'Take as long as you need. I'll cover you for five, if you wanna take longer.'

'Thank you,' I say. He leaves and I look at Gerald. He's wiping tears from his eyes from jokes we were telling that I don't remember anymore.

Gerald has a smile a mile wide. So do I.

'Ah, you young people,' he says, chuckling. His coughs come again, angry things that smother him for a moment. He takes deep breaths that exude heat. He scratches his chest, and I see red marks from how much he's been doing it. Push it out of my mind.

'We aren't all bad,' I say. He smiles, and I hug him. I don't know why. It feels right to do. I think about a lot of things with my arms around him. None of them seem as important as just holding him.

'Hey, you were infantry. We don't cry.'

'I'm not,' I say. I wipe my eyes on the back of my hands. He does the same.

'Men don't cry,' he says.

'Tell that to everyone else,' I say. I leave not long after. The whole drive there, my eyes are sore. Something painful behind them, stripping them raw. I think of how I don't have work tomorrow. I think about that, and think about how I'd caused a scene at *Rosie's* and Sarah and Liv. I realize I can't drink there. I see a motel out on the highway. Could stay for the night. There's a bar next door, across a vacant lot. I decide to. Can't think of any reason not to. Not even partly. A small woman sits behind a reception desk made of oak. Her hair is thinning and gray. It costs me thirty dollars for the night, and I take a rust colored key for room 4A and sit on the bed in silence for an hour. I hear rain approach. Feel the static in the air. I listen to it gently on the windows. My friend would be dead soon. Couldn't stop that, like I could never stop the rain. It was just as inevitable. I take off my jacket, walk to the bar. The gravel underfoot makes the sound of bones being stood on.

The bar doesn't have a name, as far as I can see from outside. A red neon alligator sits in the window, though. I presume that's what it's called. *The Alligator.* I don't know. A young man with a pockmarked face stands outside, smoking. He glares at me, nervously. I think about what secrets he has, before deciding it didn't matter. I was going to drink. A lot. My friend was dying. I can't stop it. Can't stop anything.

The bar floor is sawdust filled – all I can smell, save alcohol and the faint and distant tones of sweat. Underneath all that is some kind of regret, and the damp smell of the rain outside. A single pool table is at the back – the covered lights make a halo on the table. Pair of old biker looking heavies is playing pool, whilst a woman in a black fur coat sits at the bar. Something in a glass flute, cloudy. I see she's staring listlessly at the TV – for a heartbeat, I think she's Christy. She's not. No tattoos, older. Something faded behind her eyes, like the onset of a blindness of the soul. A couple bartenders are looking at the news, talking about acts of violence in Africa. Some kind of coup. They're interviewing a young American doctor based there – beady, sharp eyes of ocean color, black hair short and pushed back from his face. His stubble shows his age – a young man, who can't even grow a beard. A card shows his name is Richard West, M.D, P.H.D. He apparently studied at Miskatonic University, near Arkham in Massachusettes. Hear nothing but ghost stories about that place. Places out that way had a bad rep. The government raided some places around there, once. Salem, Arkham. A little fishing village, whose name had been lost, and the place had become buried at the coast. Places like that – they grow old with the sea.

'I, yeah. They, ah, the, ahm, there's a lot going on over here.' He pushes his glasses back up his nose. The air around him shimmers with heat, and I see African soldiers holding AK's with black polymer stocks and hand guards. I take a seat at the bar, and a bartender comes over. Older guy with hazel eyes. He seems angry to still be breathing. The world can make you like that.

'Getcha?'

'A Bud.' He nods, not smiling. Richard West looks around at the sound of gunfire, static pops some distance away. It carries on the wind.

'Some kinda world, huh?' says the woman. She looks oldish, wise. Something of a Latino air to her, her accent. I nod, and the miserable bastard behind the bar puts the bottle down in front of me. Richard West turns back to the camera.

'There's a lot of folks, ahm, getting hurt out here. You know. Bad things keep happening. Ahm.' He looks at the camera a couple times as he speaks. Something shy, approaching nerves. I hate to think he's sewing child soldiers and U.N troops back together. The man looked a borderline nervous wreck. The woman sat at the bar finishes her drink.

'Andy, another?'

'Sure, Ivonne.'

Ivonne looks at me, as Richard West rushes off to take the pulse of a man nursing a gunshot wound on his face, and the feed cuts back to American studios, fake lights.

'Look like you've had a kinda night.'

'Yeah,' I say. I sigh a little, something approaching a laugh but stumbling at the end. 'Yeah, I have. Couple of those kinda days, too.'

'I know the feeling.' She lights up a cigarette. I guess there's no smoking ban here, and I do the same.

'You look different than the kinda guy stumbles in here at night.'

'I wouldn't know.'

'Been to Portland?'

'Yeah. Obvious?'

'America has a heartbeat. You listen closely enough, you can hear the rhythm. It's easy enough to make a note of it, where the obvious steps are. Like the chorus of a sad, soulful song.'

I look at her with a smirk. Don't know where that came from. The way she spoke was like something beautiful in a way other than words.

'That's a very eloquent way of putting it.'

'Nah. Just know a thing or two,' she says with a coy smile. She puts her hand out, adorned with rings. Nicotine stained. 'Ivonne.'

'Joel,' I say, shaking her hand. We sit there, watching the TV. We drink.

'You have anyone special back where you're heading?' She asks.

'I...yeah. Maybe. I, I think.'

'She must have an old soul,' Ivonne says, looking at the TV. *White Claudia* had been found in a drug raid in Crooks Hollow. I shake my head. Children in handcuffs, because angry cruel people peddle the means to destroy lives for profit. I feel a quickening in my heart. Monsters are everywhere.

'She does. I think she just, well. I think maybe she's hurting. In a bad place.'

'Sounds like someone lost in the long cold night.'

'You aways talk like that?'

'Only when in good company. Drives the men I fuck crazy.'

'Oh.'

'Yeah. Shallow as a stone pond, men.' She raises her hands from the bar top for emphasis. 'The world needs oceans. Keep everything buoyed.'

I nod. I agree in a way. I hear rain against the windows, pattering against the stones outside and the cars parked there.

'We do try,' I say. 'It must be the same with some women, too.'

'I don't fuck women. Wouldn't know. People are all these locked little haunted houses, rooms of decisions and thoughts.'

I nod. She makes sense in this absurd way. I often find myself a disadvantage when conversations are like this. I'm not filled with beautiful sentiments. Oceans of thought. Knowing everything. How to act. I don't know.

'I feel like you're a little jaded,' I say. 'Like maybe once you didn't think like that, and someone made you.'

'Maybe,' she says with a smile. She finishes another drink. Stands up. I smile and nod at her. There's a sad smile playing across her face, something dark. It doesn't ease as she speaks. 'Maybe once upon a time, America and the whole world made sense. Then it snapped its jaws tight, left a wound.'

'Maybe a deep one,' I say.

'One that won't grow back into a heart.' She touches me gently on the shoulder. Kisses me once, softly, on the cheek. Whispers into my ear.

'Maybe, one day, you allow a little light into that girl's heart.' I smile, confused a little, and she leaves. Stands in the rain for a moment, and then vanishes into it. I never see her walk into the rain – she merely disappears. Ivonne. Someone with a wounded heart.

'Hey, buddy,' Andy says. 'Ivonne said to leave you her tab. Want another?'

I look at the closed door, hear the rain. Smile at a stranger who wasn't there anymore. I look at the old wooden shelves illuminated by dim electric lights. I feel like something magical has occurred, some meeting only possible at the periphery of chance and luck.

'I don't actually know,' I say.

*

PINE OAKS, OREGON
9:30 AM

I wake up with no headache, for once. I don't get out of bed, though. I think for a time, staring up at the cream mottled ceiling, the fan turning casually. I hear, distantly, the roar of an engine when it kicks into gear. I close my eyes. I look over to the mini-bar, next to the brown oak desk that holds on it an old TV. Looks like the place hasn't been renovated in years. I'm fine with it.

I go over to the window, helping myself to a beer. I check my watch, happy I have a quiet two hours before I need to set back out to Pine Oaks. I think about giving light to people. I don't know if I ever have. I suppose not – I turn away from the window at that thought, drink half the Bud in one.

I sit on the edge of the bed; run my hands through my short brown hair. It had grown back quickly. I go to the bathroom, take a razor to the sides of it. It resembles the crew cut I had in the old days of M16's and sand. I go back, finish the beer. Stare at the blank TV screen, the way the dust motes in the air danced in the light of the rising warm sun. I look at my knuckles, the bruises beginning to fade. I roll a coin across my knuckles, a trick I've had since my youth. Occasionally, as the coin passes the bruises, I feel a tingle of pain along the edges of the wounds. Just enough to feel.

I get my t-shirt back on, head to reception and pay. I head outside, lighting up my second to last cigarette, when I see Ivonne. She is stood in front of, I'm presuming, her door. I don't know. When she sees me, she smiles, waves a hand to bring me over. I look up at the greying, rain filled sky. It was pregnant with a storm – it would birth soon. I nod and smile, all those normal things, and head over.

'You going?'

'I am. Thank you for letting me use your tab.'

'It's fine. I'll get someone to pay it for me.'

'Oh, really?'

'Yeah. I've been at this a while.'

I nod. We stare at the woods opposite the road leading out of the motel. It resembles something from a dark fairytale – something to get lost in. A place where the light died between the branches.

'You wouldn't think it was sunny an hour ago,' I say. Ivonne says nothing. She smiles, which says enough. We look out into the forest. She inhales deeply, and the smoke in the air dances as if to a rhythm.

'You know, when I was young,' she says, 'I...well, I remember this story when I was young. My mother would tell it to me. Back in Mexico.'

'I don't remember any stories, from when I was a kid. Except my pa thought the sun wouldn't rise one day after a bottle whisky after a day on the ranch.'

'Might be right yet,' Ivonne says, smiling. Her eyes stare through the woods, something beyond. I think she's looking into a memory.

'The story was about a...a tailor. He, ah, he...what was it? He had no money. To feed his family. That was it. My mother used to make clothes for people in the village. That's it. This tailor, in the story, he makes a deal with the devil – A sack of gold, in return for a sewing competition...I, I think that was it. The devil, if he won, would get the tailor's soul. So the tailor threaded the devil's needle with long thread, and his with shorter thread. The devil's kept getting tangled...so, the, ah, the tailor won.'

'What did he win?'

'The thing everyone sells their soul for. Money.'

Inhale. Plumes of grey, incensed smoke. Her eyes focus again, and she blinks twice.

'I think there's something to that, still, these days.'

'I don't know.'

'I think it proves that, for money, people can trick the devil himself. I know that's not the message, or...or anything.' She stamps the cigarette into the ground, before smiling at me. She touches my arm gently, speaking not to me, but through my eyes.

'You go and tell that woman you love her. Show her that we wouldn't all trick the devil,' she says. She turns, heads to the bar. She stops halfway to it, before turning with a sly, knowing smile.

'Or, at least, we wouldn't get caught doing it.' She lowers her gaze, still smiling. Steps into the bar. It's almost as if she disappears into the gloom, and is swallowed whole. I watch the doorway for a time, before stamping my cigarette out and heading home.

*

The rain has become a bitter gown that hung over all. I stepped out into something Noah once built a boat to avoid. I look up at my apartment, before looking at the ground for a moment. I'd check home, first – I'd been gone a day. The world may have ended, and I wouldn't have known. I'm halfway upstairs when I wonder how much truth there is to that. I think about what to say to Christy – then I realize, when I see her door, how little it would ever mean. I slow as I reach the top of the stairs – tension in the air. Like a ghost of violence – the calm after something terrible is almost tangible. I remember feeling that in the desert towns and villages – the smell of cordite let the violence in the air cling to you. I smelled no cordite, but felt the tension the same.

I look at the kicked in door to Christy's apartment, and think. Something leaves me for a time – some kind of weightlessness in my heart. It's like I don't feel anything, as I push the door open softly. It creaks on hinges made of rust, and there is gloom in the room. The blinds are drawn. Her table is thrown over, the TV on the floor in ruins. The couch has been turned out – the pillows are still on the ground.

'Christy?' I say to nothing but the void. I walk past a shattered glass vase on the floor, and see the neon sign from the wall thrown against the fridge. I feel adrenaline in me, and for a brief moment, as I approach the bedroom, I feel the rifle in my hands again. Something made of steel, of engineering. Something to end something else. I resist the urge to kick in her closed bedroom door, and I quietly open it.

The room is destroyed. The bed is flipped upside down. The bedroom window is smashed – it faces away from the main street, into the inner courtyard garden. No one ever goes in it. It resembles jungle. Her clothes are all over the floor, and I spot, faintly on one wall, a small spray of blood. My mind goes to a strange place. I don't remember going next door to my apartment, ignoring the blinking lights of the answer phone machine. I remember dialling the police.

'Hello, Pine Oaks Police?' A woman with a raspy voice says.

'I, I think I need to report a crime,' I say. *Christy kisses me gently.*

'Okay, sir. Are you in immediate danger?'

'No, my, my neighbour Christy. Her, her apartment was broken into. I live at Elm Street Apartments.'

'Okay, sir, I need you to remain calm. Is there anyone in the apartment now?'

'No,' I say.

'Well, I'll see ya later, big guy,' she says.

'Little lady,' I say back. She kisses me on the lips, then.

'No one is, uh, in it. My neighbour is missing.'

'Have you entered the room?'

'Yes ma'am.'

'Did you touch anything?'

'The door and the bedroom door,' I say. I feel my knees go out, for a second. Have to put my hands on the counter. I feel like the ground has opened up and throw me into a thresher of steel teeth.

'Okay, sir, which apartment?'

'22A,' I say. 'She lives in 24A. Her name is Christy.'

'Okay, sir. We'll be right over.'

'I'll be outside,' I say. Everything is a dream – me putting the phone down, staring at it for a moment. I wander through the dream to outside my door, and stand in the doorway, waiting till I hear the sirens.

It's just a dream, I say to myself. It's just a dream.

*

The men and women in uniform come and go. I stand in the hallway with a couple of them, none of them saying anything. The mantra of it being a dream faded when I saw the first evidence bag – a cracked piece of mirror, a few spots of blood on it.

'I didn't look there. In there,' I say idly. I don't feel anything. The cops look at me with sad, stern faces. One of them has a badge that says Colter.

'It's okay, buddy,' Colter says. The other one, I don't see his badge. I nod, and he nods back.

'Yeah, she'll have just booked out. Sometimes, you know, hookers, they, you know, skip town.'

It takes everything I have, everything I am, not to hit him. I've never needed such strength. People think it's a weakness, not to strike someone – it's not. Sometimes it takes all that you are.

'She wasn't a whore,' I say. 'She was a stripper at *The Pearl Palace.*'

'Ah. Okay, I'm sorry, mister.'

I nod. Breathe slowly. A four count.

'It's okay.' I see another officer come out, her red hair collar length. Her eyes have shades of green stained glass. Her name is Farrows. She has something of a demeanour to her – as soon as she speaks, I can tell she's the boss.

'Hello, are you Joel...Joel Crowe?'

'Yes ma'am.'

'My name is detective Sara Farrows. I was wondering if you could come with us, answer a few questions?'

'Yes ma'am,' I say. I start walking, in my dream, and don't remember arriving to the police station. I'm escorted from the car, not in handcuffs. I think they wanted to give me a specific day to give a statement, but I don't remember. I remember going there, all the same. I might've argued. I don't know.

I walk through the police station, where a man sits with a blood-slicked nose. Another chair, and a woman I recognize vaguely, shivering on street corners, rocking. Her skin is the color of ash, and I see beads of sweat from the withdrawal. I see another two men fighting, being restrained by other officers.

I decide in that moment that nothing ever makes sense unless you force it to.

I'm led into an interrogation room, where detective Farrows seemingly appears in my dream. A camera is there, along with Colter. He stands against the wall, arms folded. He nods at me, that same sad smile on his face. I see he once must've worn a wedding ring, judging by his tan. He knew what it was like, then, to lose something vital to keeping you whole.

'Interview Joel Crowe,' Farrows says. She holds a folder in front of her, and the walls are the same color as the sky outside. Grey.

'So, Joel,' she says. 'How did you know Christy...' She rifles through papers. I look at the camera, whilst she does so.

'Christy...Hollows.' Farrows looks at Colter. He nods, and Farrows turns to me.

'We were neighbours,' I say. I feel that weightlessness in my heart. I wonder what I'm feeling, and if I can put a word to this empty. This sunken thing living in me. 'We were kind of dating, too.'

'Right,' Farrows says. More papers. I look at her, rest my arms on the desk.

'How well did you know her?'

'I knew enough. Know enough. I know enough about Christy to know she's not taken off, or, or run away.'

'Why?'

'She was saving money to go back to Texas.'

'Okay.' More paper scanning. Farrows's brow furrows and she closes the file. I feel a little of the tension leave her. She talks to me like a person.

'Look, Joel, I get you must've liked her.'

'I like her. Stop using the past tense.'

'Sorry, Joel,' she says. She smiles at me understandingly before continuing.

'I...I did a little checking on you. Army, huh?'

'Yes ma'am.'

'What were you in?'

I go silent for a moment. A pause as machine gun fire filters through my ears. I hear the whistle of it in the breeze.

'Infantry.'

'Where'd you serve?'

'Afghanistan. Iraq, too.'

'Ah.' She leans forward. 'First Marines, myself,' she says. I nod at her.

'Yourself?'

'First Brigade. Tenth Mountain. Then other places,' I say.

'Ah. Hear good things about them. Got a lot of medals. '

'We do okay.'

'So you were wounded, huh? I noticed the limp.'

'It comes and goes. AK took a chunk of my leg. Stitches and pins.'

'Hack job.'

'Yeah.'

'Huh.' She looks at me for a moment, trying to read my eyes. She looks back at Colter. His expression is difficult to read. Farrows looks back at me.

'Has, has Christy ever talked about being in trouble?'

'No,' I say. In my mind, already, I'm piecing things together. I'm trying to find something. Something for me. 'No, just the usual stress. She was, like I say, wanting to go back to Texas.'

Farrows nods at me again.

'You're sure?'

'I, yeah. I, I...she might've had trouble at work. Someone called, uh...Olive. Like the...the pizza toppings.'

'Okay.' She nods at me. 'Anyone else?'

'She mentioned a "Tony." Only a couple times. Never in good spirits.'

'Okay.' She turned to Colter. 'Can you have a look at current staff at *The Pearl?*'

'Shouldn't you have done that already?' I ask. My head is filled with gunfire. I remember once I was in a police station, *while my son lay in a morgue with his life shredded from him. His body was filled with glass and the impact of the world as we crashed into it.* I'm not thinking.

'I'm sorry,' I say. Farrows nods. I realize she too may have the thoughts I do. Maybe she just hides them well. Maybe in a stone wall, chains of steel. Like a creature from a fairytale – she buries the war inside her.

'It's okay. We thought we'd talk to you first, before we went out to the usual things. Okay?'

There is something warm to the tone of her voice. That quiet inflection of understanding. 'Okay,' I say. I turn to the camera.

'I'm sorry.'

Farrow smiles at me for only a frame of a second, a quick thing at the corner of her mouth.

'It's okay, Joel.' She looks at me with a sincere smile. 'Do you know anything else?'

'No, ma'am. I'd say if I did.'

'Okay, Joel.' She nods. 'Okay. That'll do. Thank you, Mr Crowe.' Colter turns off the camera and I stand. Farrows goes over to Colter and stands, talking for a moment in hushed tones. I don't hear what they say, and it's only for a second. Farrow turns and smiles as she walks past, whilst Colter disassembles the camera from the tripod. Farrows opens the door for me, and I stand there looking out at the rest of the station.

'I'll walk you out,' she says. 'Unless you want us to drop you off? Save you walking.'

'No ma'am. Need the air.'

We walk silently, and I feel like I notice my limp now more that she's noticed it. Stupid.

As I reach the front door, she speaks.

'I wouldn't go anywhere for a little bit, if that's okay. Just in case we need some more questions answering.'

'I might need to go to Portland. Providence MCU. My friend is dying.'

'Oh.'

'I'll let you know, though.'

'Okay, Joel.'

I reach for the handle, open it up to the world. The breeze carries nothing but the cold. I turn to Farrows, see she's already started walking.

'Marine,' I call. She turns. 'Semper Fi.'

She smiles.

'Hooah,' she says as she goes. I go back into the world, wondering how dangerous I felt. Scared of the answer, if only for a heartbeat.

*

I head back to my apartment on foot, watching rain dance on the mountains. I think about Christy. How she cried when I left the last time. I close my eyes, sigh. I put my hands in my jacket, and remember how she had held me. My thoughts drift to Alice. The things I said before I drove with Wyatt to Crooks Hollow. How they made no sense, even to me. I walk feeling nothing. I expect rage, but get something colder. Olive. Tony. It was something to do with that.

No. No. I do this properly. The police will handle it. She'll be fine. They'll find her, and the person who took her. It won't be like Wyatt. It won't. It won't.

A PLACE TO BURY HORSES

I sit in a police station in Portland, still with my arm in a sling. My head is bandaged, and the gauze at my back is crimson at times like the wings of a red dragon. I keep seeing Wyatt, when my eyes unfocus. The way he was in his seat, still. It's raining. I can't see anything from the blood on my face, and I know not all of it is mine. My breathing feels like shards of glass. I spit blood.

I stagger out, and the rain muffles Ray shouting at me. I hear whistling. My leg feels damaged again, but I don't care. I fall in the mud, my ears ringing.

'Wyatt?'

My thoughts are disturbed by the officer who enters the room. My eyes focus on his face, but I don't register anything. I don't remember what he looks like.

'Joel Crowe?'

'Yes.'

He says a name I don't remember. He looks at me with sad, broken eyes. I presume he saw the photo of Wyatt.

'I know this is a difficult time.'

'Thank you.'

'I just want you to know, we...we're looking for him. He called the cops, so, you know. We can find him. We're gonna. He just...he...'

'He got scared and drove off into the rain when he realized he killed my son.'

Silence. I see the lights of Ray's car as he drives away. I sit down in the mud, knuckling blood from my eyes. The officer looks at me with something deeper than sorrow.

'I mean it, we're gonna.'

'I don't know.'

Later, when I've healed, I'm driven home to Alice. She spends a month crying. We sleep in separate places. I go to the guest room. She takes ours. When I feel alone I go to Wyatt's room, and bring Mr. Bear to my chest and I breathe in the scent of my son.

It's unexplainable, how I feel. There are no words. Alice starts to drink. I save enough money to leave Portland. I fill out the papers, as does she. There is nothing more to be said.

Two weeks after, they tell me they caught him. Officer Ellis is sat across from me, my eyes unfocused because I don't sleep anymore. Feels like I'm always dreaming.

'We got him. His licence plates got picked up. He went home, apparently.'

'He wanted to be with his family,' *I say.*

'He probably didn't think he had that long left,' *she says.*

She nods. At this point I've already moved out to Pine Oaks. I go to the trial. Alice and her family are there. I sit in the dock all the same. I recount as much as I remember.

'All I could see was blood. I couldn't see Wyatt anymore.'

Ray Corfe cries. So does Alice. The rest of the life I've had between then and now is a blur of repetition and blackouts. I drink more. I lose time. I feel nothing, after a time. I think I've drowned what made me a person.

By the time I've reached the apartment building, I'm crying so much I can't see anything. I'm thankful for the rain. It hides it all too well.

*

PART FOUR:

PRAYING FOR RAIN

PINE OAKS, OREGON
10:30 PM

I feel something in my heart. I can't explain what it is – maybe it is akin to the snow in my dying friend's lungs, or the space left by a missing, beautiful person. Maybe it is filled with the way that young children died through men. The way that across the world, all around the world – in America – everything could tear itself apart.

I sit with my back against my fridge. I rack a round into the 1911, and then eject it. I go through a full clip like this. I lay in a sea of bullets. They glint as if they were gold. I lay on my side, as the world caved in. I would write, tonight.

I realize, though, that there is horror in everything. Men write about monsters, both man-made, and natural. There is a horror, however, to everything.

I sit back up, against the fridge. I scoop handfuls of golden death back into the magazine, place it in the pistol grip. I think for a time.

For one dangerous, long moment – one that stretches into an hour, the seconds become as a minute – I think of how long it would take someone to find me. If I place the gun behind my ear – as I do now – it would sever my spinal cord at the base of my skull. I wouldn't even register pulling the trigger. It's the only sure fire way. Ask anyone.

Gun behind my ear. Listen to the rain and the occasional swelling noise of passing cars. I see streetlights bleed through the window. I think for a time, eyes closed.

My finger isn't in the trigger guard. It lays flat along the slide, like that time before. I sigh, stop. Breathe something akin to night from my lungs. I still breathe, though. That's the way. I pull on a t-shirt, an oversized flannel shirt. Boots, jeans. I feel the warmth of the night cut through the rain, even through the window.

I attach the holster to my belt; notice that the shirt covers it. I walk for a time, and the rain dies.

I walk past the bar that Olive and the other girls took Christy into. I feel something cold, and walk in. I have never been in here. A neon crocodile sits above a mirrored wall. The floor is sawdust strewn, and I smell something sickly sweet. It is something approaching the sweaty smell of sex, masked by an amphetamine haze. Like walking through Vaseline. The place is filled with red neon lights, Chinese decorations. It was as if the place had fallen from another world. I look at the young people on the floor, dancing to slow, noisy blues. There is the clatter and clinking of drinks glasses, like stars, or spent shells falling to linoleum. They are all young. Children, in the dark and flushed bloody red lights. A young woman falls into my side, and for a terrible moment I'm worried about the trigger of the 1911.

If the hammer cocked, and the gun jostled, there was a chance of misfire. I'd take a bullet to the foot. Not a good idea, with no papers.

I walk up to the bar, and smell the crocodile musk of wood and heady perfume. I sit on a wooden chair, look up and down the bar. Don't recognize any of them as Olive or Christy's colleagues.

More than once, as I sit there at the bar, I feel something akin to mania. I had gone mad in a world clawing at sense. I sit under neon red lights in Oregon, a loaded gun to my side. I play the part of a detective, or a knight – I'm not. A drunk awaiting the hangover to end me is what I am.

The world is red, *like when I sit on the cold wet ground, knuckling blood from my eyes whilst my son dies in the car.*

A bartender comes up to me, a young girl with blonde hair, gray eyes. The tips of her hair are blue.

'Uh, hey,' she says. 'Getcha?'

'Bud. I was kinda looking for my friends, though.'

'Oh.'

'Yeah. You seen them? Olive?'

'Ah...she comes in with the strippers, right?'

I nod.

'I ain't seen em, mister. I, ah, maybe they're at work.' She smiles at me, uncomfortable. I nod. She brings me a beer, and I sit and drink it. I stare at myself in the mirror across from the bar, and close my eyes. I feel elbows next to me on the bar, and turn to see a young woman with brown hair. A teenager. Had to be.

'Hey,' she says. Her words are slurred, drowned in what smells like vodka. I smile, trying to be polite. All at once the enormity of what I'm doing dawns on me. I went out, with a gun.

'Hey,' I say. I try and finish my beer in one gulp, but I have to swallow half. I'm not young, anymore.

'You're a little, ahah, you're a little old,' she says. She places her chin on top of her propped up hands, smiles at me with half open eyes.

'I know,' I say, finishing my beer. The girl smiles at me.

'Guy's my age don't get me,' she says. 'They just want, you know...blowjobs, and stuff, and they don't want like, a real person? Just what they see on, on movies, and, and....'

'I think you're drunk,' I say. I stand up. There is truth in there somewhere. She has learned, as I'm sure every woman has, too much too young. I leave.

A PLACE TO BURY HORSES

I'm stood outside, thinking. The moon is high, and I feel the soft coolness of rain begin to drop on me. I look up, and the moon is no longer made of bone. I'm sure it is made of silver. I shake my head.

'I'm fucking stupid,' I say. I walk back home, and I'm halfway there when I walk past a small parking lot at the side of an old, boarded up supermarket. The name has faded in time, but once read Super Save.

I see the man and the woman there, and I recognize her as the hooker. The man has a hood up, but from my view here at the corner I recognize his ghoulish pallor. The man is colored a sickly jaundice yellow, and I hear his voice, loud, over the rain.

'I can't fucking believe you Kris!'

'I ain't like that,' the hooker says. Kris says. 'It ain't like that.'

She shakes her head from side to side, high. He has her grabbed by the throat, up against the brick wall. My mind is shutting into auto-pilot.

'You took all our fucking dope!'

'I fuckin' earned it! I had to fuck people for that! Johnny, I, I'm sorry!'

'You fucking WHORE.'

A PLACE TO BURY HORSES

He hits her, and her head snaps viciously to the side.

I don't feel myself stride through the rain towards the two. *I'm with Christy on the pier. She's holding my hand.* Johnny hits Kris in the nose, and I see the dark red blood hit the floor and mingle with the rain. It looks black, in the night.

My favourite horse is called Rose, I hear Christy say. I clock in that from the street, there was an engagement distance of seventy metres. The .45 has a standard travel speed of 830 feet per second, fired from a 1911. My bullet would, potentially, hit him before the shot rang out. I feel myself slide the pistol out.

Wyatt is hung upside down in the car and I'm limping to his side. I collapse in the mud, soaking in my own blood. My boy has an expression on his face. As if, in those last dying moments, he had seen the things that live within him. He no longer had the expression of a child.

Johnny turns to me, as he drops Kris, limp, to the ground. She looks at me with wild eyes, one half closed. Her mouth and nose are crimson. Johnny doesn't see the gun, due to the rain. I think Kris recognizes me, but I don't register. I'm not here.

'Hey, man, you want to fuck her? She owes me some fucking money!' Johnny says. He turns to her, taking a step towards her prone body with a bloody fist. I don't feel the weight of the .45 as I lift it, take second pressure. It sings, twice, in the night. Loud, powerful things.

A PLACE TO BURY HORSES

The shots reverberate around the walls as though we were in church. I feel something akin to peace as Johnny falls forward in the rain. I look at the slowly spreading blood stains at the back of his leg and just above his right hip. I look at Kris, who is too drowsy from the blows. She looks at me with blood filling up one of her eyes.

'You hold me different,' I say to someone I love, but not sure if it is love anymore that I feel.

I turn, holstering the .45. She would recover a week later from the beating. Johnny would need several pins in his leg, major surgery. He would walk with a limp forever. At least, that's how it goes in my head.

I walk through a dream to the apartment. I don't even feel the tremor of recoil. I don't feel anything, and I realize, I'm lost. I think I hear an ambulance, later, in the night. I'm not sure. I spend the night writing, though I don't remember the words till the morning.

I write as if in a dream. I don't feel anything.

*

PINE OAKS

3:00AM.

I don't sleep. I throw up a couple times – not a hundred percent, not anymore, that what I saw was true. That I shot him.

I sit by the window, hearing the normal traffic. I listen to the ebb and flow of America, and go to work. Liv is back, behind the desk. Her eye isn't as bruised; but I see the cut on her cheek still. It has faded like something she drew on herself, but I still see the shimmer of a raw wound. I walk with an unusual gait, something shaky to my steps. Don't know what that is.

'Liv,' I say, not facing her. I walk past.

'Joel,' she says. She looks at her computer for a moment. She turns to me, as I go on an early walk around. 'Joel, I, uh. I'm sorry.'

'Don't be,' I say. I don't turn to face her, can't. It's just all a dream.

I see a few people, as I go around my shift – the young man, the homeless girl. They're sat together, whispering to each other and laughing. I see the beginnings of something approaching love. I wonder if they realize it'll fade.

I look out at the window, and stare at the town hall. I see people going on daily trips, some laughing, some going for dinner, or drinks. I see, in the distance, the edge of the parking lot where I may have shot a man. I don't feel anything, so I wonder if it's true. If it is, I wonder if I would still feel nothing.

I worry about the answer for a time.

A young girl, maybe five or six, runs past me giggling. She has a *Winnie the Pooh* book in her tiny hands, and her mother is running behind her, trying to catch her.

'Lucy!'

The young girl laughs, and her mother finally catches her. I smile at the two, and the mother looks up at me. She mouths the words "I'm sorry," before picking up her daughter. Her daughter waves at me with tiny fingers and a happy smile. I wave back. I watch as her mother takes her to the children's reading area, disappearing around the corner of a shelf. I turn back to the window, and see a police car pull outside. Detective Farrows is there, along with Colter and the other one. She looks up at the library for a moment, before catching sight of me in the window. She nods, before turning to the other two. Can't hear what she says. They come into the building, and I wonder as I walk to the entrance whether I had washed off the GSR last night. If it happened.

Farrows smiles at me, but I recognize her expression as one of broken promises and a thinly stretched love. Colter is looking at Liv with a sad smile, already taking mental pictures of her bruises in his head and no doubt wondering, one day, if Liv would be on a mortuary slab. The other one simply looks at me. There is nothing to his gaze. I wonder if he, like me, feels nothing. Perhaps the world has taken that from him. Colter says something to Liv, who stands up, before pointing at me with a furrowed brow.

'That's him,' I catch her saying. Farrows doesn't look at Liv. She smiles at me instead.

'I know,' she says. Takes a step towards me. I think I feel panic, but aren't too sure. I think panic has been burned from me. I will never share that with anyone ever again.

'Joel,' she says.

'Yes?'

'We need you to come to Point Truth MCU.'

'Why?'

'We think we've found Christy.'

I feel happy, for a brief, fleeting second. I think that maybe a God has found me, and brought light back to me. Then I catch the wording, and realize this too was a dream.

'You think?'

Colter and the nameless cop look at each other for a second. Just a heartbeat too long for me to miss.

'What do you mean, you think?'

*

I'm stood looking into her room. There are machines all over her, beeping. Machines, the kind that make you breathe, sit around her. I don't recognize her face. She resembles something from a nightmare.

'I think I'm dreaming,' I say. 'There's no way.'

'Joel, I know its...it's hard, but, her family in Texas don't want to see her.'

'I.' I see the flower tattoos on her arm. I know it's her. Her face is beaten so badly that she could've been anyone. There are no words for cruelty such as this.

'Is it her?'

'Yes,' I say. It's like I admit it to myself. Like I don't believe it myself – but force myself to. Farrows wipes her face with her hand, pinches the bridge of her nose between thumb and forefinger. She hasn't slept in a while, I guess.

'When did you find her?' I ask. I lean forward, so my forehead is almost to the glass. She looks as if she has been concocted in a factory. Some monster from a poem of surgical horrors.

'We found her a few hours ago. She was on the edge of the bank by Cedar Creek River. She...well, Joel. She might not...'

'Don't,' I say. *I feel her hand slip mine days ago, as we walk home from the pier. She stands on her tip toes and kisses me.* 'Don't.'

'Joel, do you know if...'

'What happened to her?'

'I...'

'Please.'

I focus my eyes on what is left of Christy. Bloody drool spills down from the tube in what is left of her mouth to down a barely held together jaw. A nurse in the room wipes it, before checking the beeping heart monitor by her bedside. It shows faint, barely existent mountains, and flat, empty plains in between, carved of green light.

'She's been beaten by something blunt. A baseball bat, or a...a hammer. She has lacerations to her skull; some of the blows were so fierce. Her skull cracked along the edges. Dislocated jaw. She is covered in bruises, and there was...well. Joel, do you – '

'Some of the bruises are old,' I say. I don't know why. 'She got them the other day at work.'

'Oh.'

I feel something akin to hate. But as before, it bleeds from something of fire to ice. A deeper kind of hate. The kind as of a burrowing worm in the cold of a grave.

'Joel, we're going to solve this. Do you know anyone who could've wanted to do this?'

'Maybe God. Something with more control than us.'

'Joel.'

I turn to her. I don't realize I'm crying till I see her reach for a pack of Kleenex in her jacket pocket. I dab my eyes, before placing the tear flecked thing in my pocket.

'She had problems at work,' I say.

'What kind of problems?'

'I don't know.'

'Okay.' She places a hand on my shoulder. 'It's okay. She works at *The Pearl Palace,* yeah?'

'Yeah.'

She gently rubs my shoulder before letting go. I look at Christy, and turn to Farrows.

'Can I see her?'

'Of course.'

'Can she hear me?'

'I...I don't know.'

A PLACE TO BURY HORSES

I walk into the room, and the nurse has a weary look on her face, like she held a great many stones on her back. I guess maybe doctors and nurses do. I step over to the side of her bed, the room reeking of disinfectant. I look at what is left of this woman. I take her hand. It is limp, and as though she was made of nothing.

I don't say anything. I stroke her hand, not sure what I'm feeling anymore. I wonder if I've lost it – finally, the war has caught up to me, burned out what was left. I put her hand to my mouth, and kiss the back of it.

Farrows drives me home, explaining to work I wouldn't be in. I stare out of the window the whole drive back to Pine Oaks, watching as trees pass. I feel numb, and I feel, too, how I make Farrows feel.

'You know,' she says, 'when I got back, things were...weird. Like, there's a big thing about, like, how soldiers go all crazy, after. You know, PTSD, things like that. It's not...it's not like that though, is it?'

'No,' I say. I don't turn to her. 'It's not like that at all.'

'I'd say it's like...you come back, and everything is all "what has changed?" and "who are these people?" It's like they're the people you know, but, like...they're not, anymore. Like you know, deep down, you're not the person you were, and time has done something to everything else. It's like, it's not...it's your world still, but different. '

'Is there a point to this?'

'I worry sometimes, though. That, like...my husband, you know, my kids. They were there for me, when I came back from over there. I did my time, and they had to help me get back to...well, this.'

'I'm still not following.'

'War changes people, at least, sometimes. The point is...Joel, what's happened to Christy is terrible. It's...it's something wrong. But, you, you aren't...if you need help, you can ask.'

'Okay.'

'Don't...don't do anything, Joel. Leave it to us. The system works.'

'It worked for Point Truth,' I say. 'That was a soldier, too.'

'Exceptions to a rule don't break the rule.'

'It does, when exceptions have M4 assault rifles and heads full of bad dreams.'

'Do you? Have bad dreams, I mean?'

'Sometimes.'

'Of the war?'

I think for a time.

'No,' I say. 'I have nightmares about coming home.'

We pass a sign for Pine Oaks, and I see the forests begin to ebb away to the town. Farrows is silent, thinking. She chews her lip when she thinks. She drops me off at the apartment building, but doesn't unlock the car.

'Are you going to be okay?'

'Yeah. If you have any questions, I want to...I'll, you know. I'm here.'

'Okay, Joel.'

I turn to leave, reaching the handle, before turning to Farrows.

'Officer, a friend of mine at work said a guy got shot in that parking lot next to the Super Save. Is that true?'

She looks at me, with a furrowed brow.

'I haven't heard anything.'

'Would you tell me if you had?'

'Probably not. I can say, though, I haven't. One vet to another. I haven't heard anything about a shooting, though I've been busy with this, really, since they found her last night. Why?'

I go for the handle again, feeling shaky.

'Because if you had, I'd think the world made sense for once, you know?'

'I...' she starts, but doesn't finish. I step out into a sunny day. I feel my mind scream at me how I'd gone insane. It was that simple – a final truth so clear and resolute it was like blood on water. I'd lost it.

I was finally being that dangerous thing I had looked at hiding from myself. I walk to my apartment, numb, and get blind drunk. I don't remember anything. I pass out on the floor. I don't dream.

I think, as I lay there, as I black out, that I feel calm about finally losing my mind. Like a long time coming – a punch line written in blood in the desert stands, in an abandoned parking lot, in the brutalized face of someone I love.

You've gone crazy. Its okay, I tell myself. *You'll blend in with the rest of them, now.*

*

PINE OAKS

5:00 PM

I sit in a daze in my room. It's like time bleeds together. It's that intangible thing, when you get old. Years bleed into years. You wouldn't understand, unless you've been through it.

I think for a long time. Woke up an hour ago – the man I shot, I might not've. Might've imagined it. My thoughts are fractured – scents on a breeze. Like the way the summer is lost to winter. I think of Christy's smile, the way it bleeds to Alice's. They smile the same. They smiled the same, should I say. I think, sometimes, in that long quiet night – like I am now, about how Christy used to smile.

It was a casual thing, an inflection at the corner of her mouth. You wouldn't be able to tell if she was smiling. Not if you weren't looking. Just like Alice.

It was the thing that arose after a kiss, when you open your eyes and see her looking down, eyes closed, that casual smile. Something born of the warmth that a kiss could bring. Like snow melting in fire.

I snap back to being me, not noticing I am rolling a coin across my knuckles, staring at bullets. I shot someone in my imagination. I made it up. I wonder about how someone like Christy could deserve that. I wonder about cruel men and women. I wonder about me. I'm already picking up the phone before I realize I am. I've punched in the number for *The Pearl Palace* and have the receiver to my ear. I googled it after I dropped Christy off. Seems so long ago.

'Hi, you're through to *The Pearl Palace*. Our opening hours are 8:30PM till 6:00AM. If you're wanting to book a party, leave your name and number a-'

I hang up. Eight thirty. I had the day left. I don't know what I was thinking. I wanted to shoot, though. Had work at twelve till eight. I wouldn't have enough time. I call up the reception at work.

'Hello, Pine Oaks Public Library. Liv speaking, how may I help?'

'I can't come in today.'

'Um, Joel?'

'Yeah.'

'Okay, ah...look, if, if it's something to do with us sorta arguing, it's like...we're okay. We've noticed that like, you've been off a little bit lately, and, uh.... You know. We're okay, though. '

Her tone says the opposite. I don't say anything – let the sentiment simmer. I sigh, close my eyes. I'm sorry, Gerald. I need to.

A PLACE TO BURY HORSES

'My friend is dying, I need to see him.'

'Oh, oh my God. Joel, I'm sorry. I, I...'

'It's alright. No problem. I just can't come today. I'll, I'll be good for tomorrow.'

There's a conversation that happens then. I don't remember. Nothing meaningful. I needed to go to the club tonight. Olive. She knew. I'll ask her.

I sit and wait. I watch TV, write some more. By the time it reaches Eight, I'm three fingers of whisky and a bottle of Bud in. The night holds a dangerous reprieve. I feel something akin to fire over my heart, as I step out into the cold rain.

*

<u>OUTSIDE OF ROME, OREGON</u>
<u>8:00 PM</u>

The night runs past in long stretches either side of my car. Like the world had been dunked in an ink well. I think about a few things, as the world begins to droop and sag from the booze. Drunk driving. One wrong move, it'd be like Wyatt all over again. Stupid. Should know better.

I feel like people were due for a grave. I reach a comfortable speed of 60, keep my eyes open for the sign. I see the sign, and pull over – suddenly, I'm bathed in neon red and pink by the sign outside. I look up at it, thinking. My breathing is erratic. The twitch in my hand is back. I look at my hand, illuminated by the red, as my fingers dance spastically. I clench my fist tight, and feel them move against each other. It subsides, ebbs away. I close my eyes, sigh. I light up a cigarette, and wait till my breathing is regular.

I left the pistol at home. Recon. If they had better intel at La Drang, a few hundred American boys would've gotten home. I step out into the night. I feel the thoughts bite my bones raw.

The bouncer from before, when I dropped Christy off those days ago, is stood there. He's big, built like a line-backer. His head has the shape of a boulder, and his eyes are tired. He yawns at me, smiling warmly.

'Alright, boy.' His accent is unmistakeably Irish. I nod, still smoking. I try and smile, and I think he realizes I'm three sheets, or there about.

'Yeah, hey.'

'Ya alright, lad? Ya lookin' a little far gone, matey.'

I nod. If he thinks I'm belligerent and a drunk, he might not let me in. Not good.

'Nah, just looking forward to a good night. My friend works here.'

'Oh aye?'

'Yeah. Christy?'

'Raven-haired beauty with those drawings scrawled o'er her, aye?'

'Yeah.'

'Good lass.'

I smile, nod. I look around the parking lot, and there are less than half a dozen cars there, save mine. It must not be busy at this time. I offer the bouncer a smoke, which he takes.

'Cheers. Dire little fuckers on me throat, though.'

'Yeah, keep saying I'll quit.'

'Aye.' We stand for a moment, till I finish my cigarette. I nod and smile at him. He does the same. He's a polite man, but with his mass and his muscles he was clearly dangerous. I'd bare him in mind. I'd need to do something about him, no doubt. As I stepped through the black metal door, I feel something close to premonition. I knew in some quiet part of myself I would be seeing that man, with hate in his eyes, at one point. I'd need to think about how to deal with him. I take a cursory glance back, when I hear him sing softly into the night. I don't catch the tune.

To the left as I head in is a reception, where a young man in a suit sits. There are coats behind him on a rack. The desk in front of him is bare, save a black phone and a computer. There is CCTV behind him, black and white grainy images. The bouncer blows smoke out into the night. I look at him for a second, and the receptionist smiles. He's young. Like he was using this for college. Perhaps he was.

'Hey, fella,' he said. I recognized something approaching Midwestern in his tone. 'You okay? First time here?'

'Yeah. I, ah. Yeah.'

'No danger. Ten dollars in.'

'Sure,' I say. I reach into my wallet, smiling as I pass him the crumpled note. The bouncer on the TV stamps the cigarette out onto the ground, crunches it into the gravel. The young guy behind the reception gives me a paper wrist band, the color solid black with a string of red pearls on it.

'I know they aren't too, ya know, pretty, but new management rules, ya know.'

'Yeah,' I say, as he clips it together. I'm feeling detached again, like I'm wandering through an opium field. Opposite the main doors is a set of black metal stairs, and a room immediately to my right. A VIP room, or some form of office. I don't know. Not important right now.

I head up the stairs and see around twenty people milling around, the women wearing things of string and leather and nothing more. Boots clatter on the ground, and I catch a song playing over the PA that is little more than electronic garbage. *Christy must've hated it here,* I thought, before that feeling of cool icy rage fills my heart and hangs a pit over my stomach. Christy.

I head over to a mirror lined bar, whilst the club is pulsing red and purple and pink. A set of stairs next to the ones I used to climb up. I surmised they went to a roof, but I didn't know. I went over to the bar, where a young girl and a young man stood in suits like they'd wear in the 40's in some speak-easy. What fucking place this was, I had no idea. It was like I'd not held on tight enough, fallen into outer space.

I look around the people for Olive, but can't see her. I clench my teeth for a moment, feel my bones pop, and the young guy comes over. His name is Jason according to his name tag.

'Hey, can I getcha?'

'Whisky.'

'Ice?'

'Yeah. I gotta drive, yet,' I say. I smile, or try to, and the kid laughs awkwardly a little as he gets my booze. I pay nine bucks for it, and as I sip it I feel the fire warm me. I close my eyes, catching sight of myself. A red light is hung over head, and the shadows are deep carves into my face. I look as though I have no eyes. I am merely a skull of red neon, and nothing more. I feel gentle fingertips on my shoulder, and turn to see a woman with blonde hair like Marilyn and steel blue eyes. She wears a red coat, and white lingerie.

'Hey there,' she says. I smile. Can't blow cover. No. Olive. Olive and Christy. No.

'Hey,' I say to myself and not the stranger, while I think of the girl who lay with little resembling her face in a hospital.

'My name is Sara,' Sara says, 'you here on your own?'

'Yeah, I, ah. Yeah. First time.'

'Oh, I like the shy ones.' Sara leans forward, and places her hand on my shoulder. Whispers in my ear. 'They're the one that like it the most.'

She breathes warmly into my ear, and I swear I hear something like a purr. I smile and chuckle to her, and she coquettishly cocks her head.

'Buy a girl a drink?'

'Isn't drinking on the job frowned upon?'

'Well, maybe I like rules broken,' she says, winking. I order her one. We sit at a booth, and talk. She gently touches the tattoo on my wrist.

'Oh, wow. I like a guy with ink, ahaha. What's your name?'

'Joel.'

'What's it mean? The tattoo?'

'It's from...well, I was in the army.'

'Oh.' She licks her lips. 'Oh.'

'Yeah.'

'Do you maybe wanna get somewhere cosier?'

'Sure,' I say. She takes me, gently, by the hand, and leads me to a long corridor that is bordered by a red curtain away from the main room. A woman who looks like a mechanic from the Fifties sits at the end. Doo-wop vibe, tall bee-hive hair. Sara turns as we walk, and winks at me. She then turns to the older lady, who I see has taken out an IPad and is tapping away on it.

'First one, Vera,' Sara says. Vera smiles at me.

'And what a first one he is,' she says. Her accent is thick, and I recognize it as a Brooklyn one from someone I used to serve with. The girl leads me into a room with a door covered in a velvet red drape. There is a single, long seat across from the door, and she takes my whisky and places it by the door on a small table. She smiles at me as I take a seat, take stock of her. She dances, and takes off her clothes to music I can't discern the lyrics of. Something about blurred lines. There is a tattoo on her rib of the lines of a heat rate monitor. I don't ask.

'Do you like what you see?'

'Yeah,' I lie.

'You know, you're a strong looking guy...I like it.'

'I like it too. Um, I was wondering if maybe Olive was here? I heard she's a good dancer.'

The girl, Sara, pouts at me, with a devious smile following after.

'I don't think Olive can give you what I can,' she says, taking a step towards me. 'No one can like I can.'

She kneels in front of me, between my legs, and runs her hands over me. I don't like being touched anyway, but I have to let it go. Christy. I need to find out about her.

Sara laughs at me flirtatiously, and kisses me on the cheek.

'I make a rule that the first guy I get in a night, I blow. You want that?'

'No,' I say. She kisses me on the cheek again, and then starts dancing. A little while later and it's over. She's sat next to me and I'm giving her a twenty. She smiles at me, and I smile back. She speaks to me as she puts the money into her bra.

'You want some more?'

'Could we talk?'

'Talking is the same amount.'

'Sure,' I say as I give her another forty.

'What do you want to talk about, sweetie?' She says as she gently taps her fingers on my forearm. After a moment, she holds my hand tenderly.

'I want to know if you know someone called Christy.'

'I, ah...' She starts, before she looks at the doorway to the room. There is the briefest play of nerves across her face. Her eyes dilate. Fear does that. She hides it, stowing it in the cargo of herself. 'I don't think so. She look like?'

'Like someone who used to work here. Smaller than me, pale. Tattoos on her arms of flowers and roses.'

'I, ah...I don't know.'

'The bouncer said she worked here.'

'I...oh shit, mister.' I start to ask her what she knows when Vera comes in. She's smiling, and looking at her IPad. She smiles at Sara, then me. She has the cold eyes of a shark. There is nothing to them, only dark. Like a dying star.

'Sara, hun, Tony got a guy needing special treatment. You follow me? Be a doll, V.I.P room two.' Vera smiles at me then. I swear her teeth are long.

'If you'd liketa follow me, my boss Tony wanna word.'

'Sure, ma'am.' I stand up, and turn to look down at Sara. There is pleading in her eyes, I feel. Something approaching a wish. I turn to Vera, and nod. I smile.

'No problem. Thanks for the dance.' I don't turn to Sara; I simply follow Vera down the hallway to a door. There is a star on it, a black one. As we walk to it, I talk to her.

A PLACE TO BURY HORSES

'Have I done something wrong?'

'Naw hun, he just wantsta ask ya somethin.'

'Sure. Good. First time here, and, I, you know, didn't want to cause trouble.'

'I know hun,' Vera says as we reach the door. She puts a hand on it, her nails chewed and broken. 'I know.'

We enter into the office, and Anthony is there. The office is cluttered, with a desk in the centre and a beautiful vase-lamp resting on it. There's a computer, and a bank of CCTV screens by a small window that shows the woodlands and a side road around the building. A beautiful painting sits on a wall of a woman bathing in a lake by the moonlight. Anthony himself is a softly featured and round man, with steel eyes and a gentle smile. His hair is short and trendy. He looks like the neighbour you'd bring to BBQ's in the summer, and would laugh at his vulgar jokes. He looks kind.

It disarms me, and for a moment, I forget why I'm here. He stands up from behind the desk, and extends his hand.

'Anthony,' he says. His accent is heavily Irish, like the bouncer. 'I hope Vera here didn't scare yeh too much?'

'Nah,' I say. I smile. Vera waits by the door, and I shake Anthony's hand. It is delicate, and cold.

'Vera, could yeh be ah dear and get me McKinney and Saskia?' Anthony looks at me. 'Yeh'll like her. Straight offa boat.' He smiles at me in a friendly way, and gestures to a wicker chair next to the desk. Not opposite, but to the side. I smile and nod and sit there while Vera leaves, closing the door behind her.

'So, I hear yeh were askin about a lass called Christy?'

A beat of silence. I wonder, idly, if he has a gun on him. At this angle, I wouldn't be able to see it. Didn't plan for this. It was all spiralling.

'I, ah, yeah. A friend of mine, Jay, he told me she's awesome. Um, and her friend, Olive.'

'Ah, Olive. Aye, great lass. This Christy though, she was the one with the flowers, aye?'

'Yeah.'

'Aye. I knew her. She quit.' He furrows his brow, before nodding. 'Aye, about...a few days ago.'

'Oh,' I say. 'That's a shame.'

'Aye. Good lass. A little dim, sometimes, with too big a heart for the customers, but aye.'

I resist the urge to hurt him.

'Yeah. Why did she quit?'

'Got caught stealing. Told her it was either the cops, or, yeh know, quitting. She chose the latter of the options.'

'I see.' Anthony nods, smiles, and looks around the office. He points to the painting.

'Yeh like that?'

'Yeah. It's, uh, it reminds me of like...I know this is weird to say, but a fairytale, kinda.'

'Aye. Yeh know the brick-shithouse yeh passed on the way in? His mam painted it. Ain't it beautiful?'

'Yeah. It's nice.'

'Aye. Brought it from the old country. Yeh know. We came over, an' found America here, and we thrived. Aye, not in a fancy way – I ain't shittin' gold, like – but close enough to make yeh forget.'

'Yeah. Look, Anthony –'

'Tony.'

'Right, Tony. Why am I here?'

He smiles at me, but there's no warmth in it. There is something to the way his eyes seem relaxed and calm that is unsettling.

'I just thought I'd explain the Christy situation before yeh got all confused and that. Better to hear it from the guy in charge then staff, yeh know? Transparency is the only thing these days. It's the only thing that doesn't get yeh properly fucked.'

I nod. There is something to this. To his words. He believes them about as much as I believe mine. Two men, sat in a dark room in a dark place, talking of transparency. A hundred years ago, this would be called progress. Now, it isn't. He nods at me and smiles.

'Gotta keep on keeping on, lad.'

I nod. There is the sound of the door behind us opening slowly. I turn my head, and Anthony smiles at McKinney and the woman stood next to him with her long hair and straight fringe and black silk clothing. The woman looks at the ground, and I recognize what she's feeling.

'Ah, McKinney! Nice to see yeh. Was just talking to the lad here. Saskia, how are yeh?'

The girl doesn't look up, but speaks with a soft Russian accent.

'I'm okay.'

'Good lass. Yeh're gonna be looking after this lad for a while, special treatment, aye?'

A PLACE TO BURY HORSES

She nods before she looks up at me with brown and green eyes. She gives me a cursory look. I wonder what she's thinking. I'll never know. Part of me wonders if she's wondering if I'm going to hurt her. I turn to Anthony.

'Ah, all the same to you An- I mean, Tony, I'm gonna go. I kinda only came for...you know, Christy or Olive.'

'Ah right,' Anthony says. He looks at me with a wry, gentle smile. He stands up, shakes my hand. He nods to Saskia, who is staring at the floor again.

'Yeh know, if yeh wanted, she'd probably let yeh have a go, if yeh get me, lad.'

I turn to Saskia, before looking at Anthony.

'I get you. No.'

'Alright lad, McKinney'll show yeh out if yeh want. Don't be a stranger though, yeah?'

'I won't,' I say as I leave. Saskia is led to a V.I.P room by Vera, who's waiting outside. McKinney leads me through the slowly forming crowd of people, and to the cool and dark night. I light a cigarette, pass him another. We stand for a time, and talk.

'Yeh know, it ain't all bad. I know, it, like, didn't seem that good, but it is.'

'How would you know?'

'Where I grew up, around Dublin-town, a lot of lasses were like that. Did this kinda stuff and worse. They get through it. I don't much like havin' to rough folks up, and...yeh know. Heh. I don't know.' He shakes his head, looks at the moon which has been covered by a slowly moving ash-grey cloud. 'I forgot what I was tryin' to say.'

'It's alright,' I say. 'I do that too.'

We stand in silence for a time. I can't over-react – I see clearly now how out of my depth I am. McKinney is a strong looking man – he could do damage. Anthony is smart, and likes himself to be a philosopher. That means he's dumb, and more than likely is packing a gun.

A combination I saw too often in the army.

I drive home, and don't put the radio on. I can't think. There has to be something, I say to myself over and over again. *There has to be something I can do.* I'm gripping the steering wheel that tight, my knuckles take on the color of the moon.

*

PINE OAKS, OREGON
5:00AM.

I don't sleep well. I think of the young woman who used to live next door. I toss and turn that night. I swear I hear ghosts of memories. Or maybe that's what dreams are. Witch haunted things made of glass and raw fire that burn and cut. Yes. Memories are worse than ghosts.

The slowly rising sun brings in rays of gold, the dust in the air dancing. I sit on my couch, staring at the turned off TV.

Have you ever seen a ghost?

Mine came to me in the dying of the night. I sit there; losing time, whilst the world turns and someone I think I love dies. It's a moment or two, but I feel a breeze to my right. I turn, and see Christy. She's not dying, not anything. She's wearing the same clothes we wore that night to the pier. I know it's in my mind. I know it. The bad thing is, so does she. She sits next to me, cross legged on the couch, smoking. She too stares at the TV.

'Hey, big guy,' she says. I stay silent. I look at my reflection on the TV. There is no one else here.

'I know, this is, ah. You know.'

'You're not here,' I say to myself. 'You're not.'

'I know. I think I'm a comfort thing.' She exhales the smoke slowly. There is only mine in the air. 'You know?'

'Yeah. I do.'

'I think you need help, beautiful. I think you do.'

'I know.'

Her hand is on the nape of my neck. Her fingers have no warmth or cold to them. She is made of nothing except the night as it fades away. I turn to her, her smile small but full of wonder and promise. I smile at this ghost in my mind.

'Please don't do something bad, Joel. Please stay good. For me.'

'Christy, what did you do?'

'I only know as much as you.'

'I should've done more,' I say. I expect a reply, but don't get one. I turn to her, but she has already faded away. She's not there. She was never really there. Just like I wasn't, in the way that mattered most. Our lives are ruled by these little tricks of memory and of the mind; ruled by nightmares. She was as close to a ghost as I know.

I sit there for a time, and remember how she kissed me. I remember how she would stand on her tip-toes, and look down after a long breathless kiss we shared once. I go over everything in my mind.

I come to a conclusion, on ghosts.

I know that the night would never end for me.

I knew this in my bones.

*

I go to work, thinking. It's something to do with the club. Has to be. The way she acted. The way *they* acted. The girl who had offered to love me with her mouth had become a statue at the sight of Vera, and the mention of Christy and Olive's name. Olive. They had argued, Christy had said. Olive had called a few times. I know there is something to the way Christy looked at her phone, the way she had talked to Olive on the phone after the pier. Olive knew something.

I walk past reception, and Liv is there. She smiles as though someone had given her the world. I smile, not one hundred percent sure if I mean it. I'm filled with something coiled and cold as if a snake of ice had nested in me.

'Hey Joel!'

'Hey there.'

'How are you?'

'Steady and even. Yourself?'

'I...yeah. I, um. Thank you, for...um. I mean, I guess thanks for the help. I, ah...I broke it off with him, again.'

'Oh, good for you. Good. I mean that, I'm, you know. Happy. For you.'

She furrows her brow at me. I think of the way Christy is breathing through a tube and that Wyatt is in the ground and that we all, always, are sometimes monsters.

'I...yeah. I...' She smiles at me. My hands are on the desk, and she touches one of them gently with her finger tips. I hear Christy whisper words I can't make out in my ear. I know it's her though. Has to be. I pull my hand back, slowly, and smile.

'I'm glad you're okay.'

'I...' she says, but I can see a few things play across her face. Confusion, a little bit of rejection. It's only there a second, but it's long enough. I nod, and then make up an excuse for going on rounds. I go to the bathroom, and stare at myself in the mirror. My breathing feels shallow, my heart arrhythmic. Something had happened, and was now passing. I feel a wave of nausea sweep over me and I dry heave into the sink. I wet my face with water from the tap, and leave. I feel calm bleed over me slowly over the next hour. By the time I finish work and the moon is out in a sliver of bone I feel better. Not all the way, but nearly. I go outside and smoke, rain a steady mist hanging in the air. I look up at lights from the building opposite, some apartment building much better than the one I stay in. I smile at seeing a baby in a window, staring with an expressionless, wonder filled face in to the world. The child's mother is laughing and picks up the baby, a phone in the crook of her neck. She holds the baby close and rocks it, before disappearing back into the room, away from the window. I never got that, I remember. Not from my father. Never gave it to my son. There is a moment of regret. I feel the wind die. *Rain.*

I'm disturbed by a man pulling up in an expensive looking car, with a stern expression on his face. He is a strong, sinewy man. I recognize the look. Next to him is another man, this one younger and whose face is scarred from acne. They look up at the library, and then at me. I nod, smile. They might be lost.

'Hey, buddy,' says the smart looking man, 'you know if Liv is here?'

'No,' I lie. 'She called in sick.'

'Ah.' The man runs a hand through his hair, before I hear the door open behind me. I feel rain on my face as I turn towards Liv. She looks at the car, whilst the guy in it stares at her. Liv takes a step back and slightly towards me. I don't know.

'Justin, what are you doing here?'

'I wanted to talk to you,' says the guy with the smart clothes. He gets out of the car, and looks at Liv. At me.

'There's nothing else to say. I gave you the ring back. I, we're over. Done.'

'Nah, Liv, listen, I, I know I –'

I don't give him chance. I know who he is now. I've stopped caring. I don't do it for Liv, or a sense of right or wrong. I take a step forward for me. I want to hurt someone. I don't know. I feel like I'm never really here.

'She doesn't want to talk.'

Justin looks at me, his friend stepping out now. There are only a few people around. I feel that icy snake bite my heart.

'Who are you, sorry?' Justin asks. I don't know, in all honesty, myself.

'No one.'

'Well, stranger, I'm wanting to talk to her. Not you. Alright? I'm not wanting trouble.'

I look at his friend. Young and nervous. Men like these are like children, in a way. Children, groping in the dark for the light. Justin jabs a finger at me quickly, before backing off a step.

'I'm not wanting trouble.'

A PLACE TO BURY HORSES

'It's no trouble to me,' I say. Justin looks to his friend. I see emotions play between them. I think they're considering options. I'm aware of Liv by the door, shaking in the slight rain whilst the air cools our breathing to mist. Keep them away from her. I'm not a knight. I know why I'm doing this. Justin looks back at me.

'Look, man, there's two of us. Please. Okay? It's okay. We're not going to hurt her, or, or anything. We're just...I'm just wanting to talk to her.'

'One,' I say.

'What?'

'There's only one person here.' I drop my cigarette on the ground. Stamp it into a dark ash stain in the rain. 'You.'

'Hey man,' his young friend says. I look at him, as he takes a step around the car. Already, I know how this will go.

'The reason there's only you, Justin, is because your friend will run away. Call the cops. An ambulance. I'll hurt you too bad, it'll scare him. He won't want to stay. He'll leave.'

Justin looks at me with wide eyes. I'm leaving a message for him. He takes another step back to the car. Good. I hear Liv move to my right, a distance behind me. Near enough back at the doors. Keep them away. They need to go. Back into their cars. I more and more have realized I really want to hurt anyone right now. Might not stay in control. Stupid.

'Go home. And on the way, forget about Liv. Me. Go home.'

They do. They get back into their car, and they drive into the dark. As far as I'm aware, they don't bother Liv anymore.

The occasional drunk dial, but nothing more. I see the car fade into the night, the dying of their tail lights as the dark swallows them. Liv is by the door to the library, looking at me. My heart is a drum, playing staccato to a rhythm of some old war song.

'Joel?'

I say nothing for a time. My breathing is slowing, returning to normal. Feel a little fire die. I realize I'm smiling.

'I'm okay,' I say. 'I'm okay.'

The world, in a small way, starts to make sense – there is escalation for everything, and everything, eventually, ends.

I sit for a time on my couch, before writing. I'm not focused, though. In my head, I hear Christy laughing. When I finish, I hear her sigh softly in my ear as I lay on my bed. The dark hides so much – it's easy to imagine her here, rather than dying in a hospital.

It's easy to imagine her here.

*

PART FIVE:

"GO BY GOD AS A

SOLDIER"

PINE OAKS, OREGON
TWO WEEKS LATER.

A half month later and there is a moment in the dawning sun where I see Alice. I don't think about the argument before I took Wyatt through to Crooks Hollow. I don't think about her and me in our summers of love and winters of warmth. It's a shimmer in the sun – a mirage. I see her, though, in the reflection. She's smiling. I haven't seen her smile in a long time.

Her hair is golden, rays of fire from the sky that surround her like a halo. She smiles in that subtle way I love, and that she loved to flaunt to me. I place my hand on the window- there. There is already the warmth of the sun. It feeds into the world, lets things grow. I close my eyes.

Gerald had died. Wasn't there for the funeral. Think there was the shame. Remember my father passing – a night in the lonesome October. Dead leaves. The beginnings of snow.

I wonder on time, for a time. I wonder what secrets he took with him. I decide there, holding a mirage and a sun-born dream, that death, for all intents and purposes, defies the natural law of things.

A PLACE TO BURY HORSES

Every person is a small cosmos of worlds – ideas, dreams, fears, doubts, loves, memories. A man much smarter than me – though that doesn't take much – said that "for every action, there is an equal and opposite reaction."

This rule applies to all life – so, by that token, death is unnatural. There is no reaction. It is the nullification of all things. A thousand worlds, dying like stars in the past, send their old photographs to us in the night's sky. There is no reaction.

I open my eyes. Feel the warmth on my face. Alice is gone. I think of my son. I wonder who he'd be by now. I'll never know. Never need to.

I get showered, shaved, go to work. My hair is longer now, and sits close to my head. I think my eyes are softer, now, too – I visit Christy twice a week. I hold her hand, tell her stories. Her heart rate is a steady rhythm. I notice she's losing weight. The doctors tell me she was beaten that badly that her brain is bleeding. They don't know when she'll wake up. Her family, as far as I'm aware, hasn't visited.

I go to the range a couple times. Like tonight.

Bones is stood by my side, whilst I shoulder the Garand. The kick-back is more manageable now. There's a jam though. I work the charging handle till the golden sliver of metal springs free. I look at the base, and see the firing pin has dented the bottom, but not primed it.

'Fuck. Damn thing better not be breaking,' Bones says. I pass him the bullet, and he looks at it. 'Like the damn thing doesn't want to shoot.'

'Wouldn't that be a world,' I say. I put in another clip, and put four rounds down range. I pretend everything wrong with the world is lined up in the sights. There's no jam then. Bones and I sit outside after, on those plastic chairs. The air is humid – a gift from the south. I think of horses for a time, till Bones returns. He yawns, before sitting down and lighting a large hand rolled cigarette. It smells of chimneys and smog.

'How are ya doing?' He asks. I nod, not really at anything. The sky is purple as the sun dies and the dark draws in.

'I'm, uh. Yeah. I'm okay. Yourself?'

'I'm alright. Noticed you were, uh. You know. Not really talking in there.'

'I just got stuff on my mind, Bones. I'm...I don't know.'

'I get you,' he says. 'I get you.'

We talk for a while. He asks me about Christy, I say I visit often. We talk about my friend Gerald. Bones asks me questions about him – what was he like, did he have any stories, was he a good man? There are others I can't answer. I realize I didn't know Gerald all the way I should've done. It hangs over my head till I leave. I feel drained, and I visit Christy again. They let me visit her whenever, really. They know better than to ask me to leave, I think.

Her face is heavily bandaged still, and her breathing is shallow. I wonder if she's dreaming, or if it's something deeper than that. Somewhere past sleep, past the conscious. I wonder if there's anyone there. I tell her about Bones, how he asks about her. I tell her about work, how the kid with the glasses has started talking to that girl who I arranged a cab for. I joke around that I've helped young love along. It takes me a moment to realize my eyes are wet and I apologize to her. I don't know why.

I go home and sit on the edge of the bed. Distantly, I hear sirens. The red light of the Chinese restaurant across the road carves deep wells of shadows. I look at myself in the mirror, the scars on my leg. I'm a little rounder than I used to be, softer. Won't do. I decide that I need to work out. I feel as if in preparation, but I don't know what for. Or maybe I do, and can't admit it to myself.

I practice loading the 1911. Too wired to sleep. I figure out how to do a press check one handed. I practice drawing it from the holster. I manage to get it smoothly down. The sun is rising now and I'm looking at the bullets on the table, the magazines next to them. The 1911 in unloaded in my hand, with the slide pulled back to expose an empty chamber. I feel renewed and of purpose. I don't know why, after this time, I feel like this. I think, maybe, it's to do with the fact I'm tired of feeling useless to the people I love. I put the pistol on the table, and smoke.

The sun bleeds in and burns all the stars away. I'd start soon. Had to. I had to, for Christy. I just didn't know how.

No. The cops. They're handling it. I'm off work today – I'll go to the station, ask. Find out something. Anything. They have to have something. Have to.

*

I arrive a little early, around 6:30 in the morning. I haven't slept and it shows. My eyes are sunken hollows, and dark rimmed. I run a hand through my short hair whilst the receptionist sits with a coffee. She's a large, old lady with brunette hair streaked with silver. She looks at her computer screen through glasses that reflect everything like the surface of the sea. She looks up at me, before her gaze falls again.

'She shouldn't be too long, Mr. Crowe. Detective Farrows is just in a meeting.'

'No problem,' I say. She smiles at me, gently. I don't know her name. She looks up at me, and puts her hands on the desk in front of her. She holds her own hands as she speaks like a caring teacher.

'You know, I know you must be pretty upset. Don't worry though young man. We'll all get through everything together.'

A PLACE TO BURY HORSES

'You Christian?'

'Yes.'

'It shows,' I say with a smile. She nods and goes back to her work, and I read a magazine about fly fishing, held in a pile on an old square wooden table. After a few moments, Farrows comes out. She is flustered – I can tell something has annoyed her in the meeting. She sees me and it does little to lighten her mood.

'Mr. Crowe. Please, follow me, by all means.' The receptionist smiles at me, and I wave at her as I follow Farrows through the doors that I was led through not too long ago.

'Thanks.'

Farrows leads me through to some kind of office room – it's different than the interrogation room, but doesn't bear her name on the door. So either she was new, or this was a new office. She sits in a brown leather swivel chair; I sit on a white thing made of wood. She rests her hands on the desk, and smiles at me. I can still see annoyance from whatever she had been in before.

'Hey, Joel. Hey. Sorry if I was a little, you know.'

'Are you alright?'

'Just a lot of stuff to arrange, you know. Having to do a conference about...well, you've seen the news.'

'That White Claudia stuff?'

'Bingo. Stuff is like brain rot. Melts folks down to bare cells.'

'Heard stories about it.'

'Yeah.'

A pause, and Farrows closes her eyes. She shakes her head, and smiles before she opens her eyes again. She's calmer, now. Took a breath.

'Anyway. Moving along. How can I help? How are you?'

'I'm, you know. Here. I was, you know. Has there been any, any update? I mean, about Christy? Did you talk to that Tony guy? Did you go to The Pearl?'

'We did, yeah. He told us she'd been stealing from customers, had to leave.'

'You believe him?'

'No. But we have to investigate. These things take time. I know that's, um, shitty, and cliché, but that's how it works. We have to have the time to do the things we...you know...need to. We'll find out, I promise, but you...we need time, Joel.'

'I know.'

She looks at me with understanding, warmth. In my mind, I know what she's saying is true. It's not what my heart says, though.

'Are you going to be okay?'

'Yeah,' I say. I know I won't. I'm tired. Maybe it's an accumulative weariness, something grafted to my bones over a lifetime. Maybe there's a crack in my soul.

Olive knew.

'Thank you for your time, detective.' I stand up, all my nerves electric. I needed to do something. Something to someone. I feel the officer's eyes burn into my back as I leave. I can't imagine how she feels – I don't need to. We're all our own little haunted houses.

'Joel,' she says. I turn, and there's something in her eyes. Something approaching pleading. She doesn't say anything else. Instead her gaze lowers to her hands, which are shaking. I leave. I walk a little down the street, when I see the black car.

It's a slow approach at first. Something bordering stalking. Then, as if a horse, it gallops down the street to me. I see the car that had dropped Christy off pull over. Anthony is there, McKinney. Vera is the driver. Anthony smiles at me, and waves at me. I nod. I feel nothing. McKinney steps out, and leans his tree trunk arms on the roof of the car. He's wearing sunglasses still. He smiles at me, in a friendly, warm way.

'Alright, lad. Can we have a quick word with yeh?'

'Depends.'

'On?'

'Content of conversation,' I say. I feel blood rising. I could dart down the alley to the left, but then I'd be out of public view. I get in, and they'd...who knows.

'It's about yeh lass, Christy. Come on, mate. Only be a minute.'

I realize I could at least try. I don't know what happened to her. I could get something out of them. Anything. I could...I could.

I could kill them.

'Sure,' I say. I play it nonchalant, but I know that they've seen me leave. Probably been tailing me somehow. Vera. Vera must know where I live, somehow. Maybe she just put two and two together, or followed me. Either way.

I walk around the front of the car, look at Vera. She's staring straight ahead with a thousand yard stare. Something to that. Maybe she wasn't that bad. Maybe not a monster. I don't care.

I climb into the back, and McKinney is sat next to me. Anthony across. The seats are of grey leather, and I smell something sweet and smokey. Could be opium. Something akin to it. Anthony nods at me, smoking. He has an ashtray built into the door next to him. I wonder, already, how stupid I am. McKinney is built too big. He'd hurt me bad. Anthony, as I knew, more than likely carried a gun. A thousand decisions and revisions of planning. My only way out would be through the front. I'd never reach it. Anthony speaks to me through an ashen haze.

'So, lad. How are yeh?'

'Fine, Tony. Yourself?'

'Aye, yeah. Yeah. I'm alright. Just wonderin' what yeh were doing in the station, like.'

'Found out a friend was in an accident. Was in the hospital. Wondered what happened.'

'Why didn't yeh go there?'

'I did.' McKinney smiles and me, nods. He whistles something musical. His mother was a painter. I try and be reassuring. I realize we're essentially going in a loop around the town square, but I don't let them know that I notice. 'I just wondered if there was, you...you know. Anything I could do.'

'What happened to them?'

'Mugging.'

'Shite, mate. That's proper shite.'

'Aye,' McKinney says. I look at him, and I wonder how hard he could hit. I think more about escape. I couldn't go back home. They knew. Even if they didn't, it felt like they did.

'So, you know.'

'Aye. So, Christy. Let's chat, aye?'

'Sure.'

'We fired her, yeh know? Or gave her the choice, anyways. I'm just sayin...men do strange things for pussy. Like it drives a current through our heads. Burns sense from us.'

I bite back hitting him.

'I know.'

'I mean, this Christy, she used to blow me workmates. Like, yeh know, business mates. She was loopy, mate. Well and truly loopy.'

Bite back.

'Ah.'

'Aye. Amount of guys who came in her mouth, wonder she could taste anythin' other, yeh know?'

He looks at me, and all at once I realize what he's doing. I attack him, self defense, then I'm lying in the street with a bullet hole. He'd get away with it. Don't let him. There's going to be a time, I realize, sat in the car with those three, that I would kill them all. Not today. Not tomorrow. I'd kill these three. I make a Faustian deal with myself.

'I see.'

A PLACE TO BURY HORSES

Anthony looks at me curiously, and I can't place what is playing across his face. For a minute, I register regret. I think he misjudged me. Thinks I'd retaliate. No. I'd bury him, hard and loud. Not a soft kill. Something that would overshadow everything he was, and leave a message for the ones who would come after.

'Im just sayin', might be an idea to leave it nah, lad. What's done is done. We haven't done anything, lad. Save let her go.'

'Why am I here, then?'

'Just in case yeh were lookin' to make shite up with the cops. It's alright – it's emotional, mate – but just so we're all on the level. Same rung of the ladder.'

McKinney looks at me, and I see a flash of something. Anthony hadn't planned for me to act like this. McKinney was going to hurt me. Unavoidable. It's fine. I need to know what he moves like.

'McKinney, walk this lad to his door?'

'Sure, boss.' He nods at me, smiles. I notice that it's artificial. Like he's learning how to be a person. 'Come on, mate. Get yeh home.'

'Thanks,' I say. I step out, realizing I'm several blocks from home and far from the police station, in an alley I only partially recognize. I barely step out into the day before McKinney hits me from behind.

It's not savage, but cold. Clinical. He strikes me above the right eye with blows that seem to bend the world around them. I feel my nose break. I manage to lash out a hit, catch his jaw, but it's glancing. It's over before I know. The last thing I see from the floor is of McKinney walking away. Can't open one eye. My nose is a dull ache. I taste blood. Cold, with the finesse of a surgeon. I realize, as I slip unconscious, that I would have to kill McKinney first, and quickly.

I cough, and feel a tooth come loose from the back. I watch them drive away, and it takes a time for me to remember to breath. My eye is the main concern. Can't open it. Not good. It's the eye I use for iron sights. I stagger to my feet, support myself with a wall of the alley. I lose track of time, and it takes a while for me to get to the apartment. On the way, I make a call.

Bones. Everything ends, and anything can end everything else.

*

McKinney's beating was raw, like a surgeon carving at the fibres of nerves. He was the danger. I knew that. My eye is still closed, and I feel my nose bones shake and shudder as I place a hand against a wall in the alley. I reach with shaky bloody hands into my pocket, get my phone. I have Bones on speed dial.

'Bones.'

A PLACE TO BURY HORSES

'Joel, hey. Hey, man. How are you?'

'Christy is dying.' I'm delirious. I wonder for a moment if the beating had bled my brain, if I would die in this alley. The world spins and goes black. I fall to my knees, which jolts me to consciousness. Fuck. Fuck.

'Joel, what? What's happened? Are you drunk?'

'I need you to pick me up from my place. It's at Elm Street apartments in Pine Oaks. Can you come? Fuck.'

I see blood on the ground in front of me, as I wipe my nose and pull back a crimson glove. There is a loose, dark vignette around my vision – something oscillating like the night. My focus is gone, too – the depth of field had become short. Everything was blurry, and contorted.

'Joel, are you okay?'

'Just come to my place. I need to go to the ranch. I can explain. Just hurry. I think I'm dying.'

'What?'

'I'm fucked up,' I say, and I drop my phone. My fingers aren't working. Beaten too badly. Focus and take count of my injuries. I try. I can't think. There's blood in my eyes, *like when Wyatt died.* I shake my head, and it feels as though there is ice on the inside of my skull.

A PLACE TO BURY HORSES

I don't remember getting to the apartment, and I'm barely through the door when I vomit. Stupid. Shouldn't have gotten into the car. Should have killed them. Taken them with me. All of us dead.

I collapse against my fridge, and the world closes into a dark Vaseline haze. I think I see Alice, again, in the dancing dust illuminated by the sun. I needed only a little more. A little more strength, resolve. Just a little more, till it's done. I cough blood up on to the floor. Can't see. Can't.

*

I wake up on the couch at Bones' place. I see his wife, with my bloody clothes in a wash basket, stood by the kitchen door. Bones has his back to me. Everything sounds distant – I recognize the distortion as one caused by concussion. My vision fades in and out. The two speak in hushed tones. I believe that Marybeth is worried about what I am involved in, what I have brought to their home shrouded in blood and tasting of the cold. I see her eyes dart to me, whilst Bones shakes his head. He places his head in his hands whilst the light dies and I dream again.

*

I wake up then properly hours later, with the faint waning light of the bone-like moon washing over all. The living room is carved in deep dark shadows, save for the TV. Clint Eastwood is walking past an old man who is sanding a coffin stood by a wooden wall. A cigarillo hangs loosely from Eastwood's mouth.

'Get three coffins ready,' Eastwood says, whilst I try and clamber to my elbows. I give up. It's too painful, and sharp steady stabs of red heat erupt over my face. I feel gentle hands, and look up with my one good eye at Marybeth. She is in her pyjamas, and faintly I smell disinfectant.

'Don't move, Joel. No. Don't, sweetie. Lay back down.'

I do as she says. My bones are metal, and weigh me to the sofa.

'What happened?'

'You called Bones. Said you were fucked up, told him where you lived – but not what number. Had to go door-to-door. Found yours with bloody handprints on.'

'Shit,' I say. My face is made of boiled flesh and glass. Least, that's how it feels. Marybeth gently touches my forehead.

'Jesus. You're burning up.'

'Feels like the whole of me is broken.'

'You're lucky. Bones found you, passed out on the floor, blood all over you. You took a beating.'

'I noticed.' I close my eye – the world has taken to spinning slightly. I open it again and the world is stable and strong.

'Joel, what's happened? The car ride here, while you were in and out, you talked about pearls, and about how Christy is dying, and it's your fault.'

I stare at the ceiling. I'm tired. Too tired. Everything hurts.

'Where's Bones?' I ask. Marybeth sighs and looks at the TV for a second, as Eastwood guns down men in front of a corral, talking of apologies.

'He went to get you some antibiotics. We're worried about your eye. I, you know, I know a little about, you know...Jesus, Joel. What's happened?'

I stare at the ceiling, and wonder at the question myself.

'I have things to bury,' I say. Car lights pour through the window, and for a brief minute everything is bathed in gold. Marybeth goes to the window, moving the blinds. She looks at me for a moment, before going over to the door and unlocking it. I didn't notice the rifle by the door at first. I do now. A Mosin Nagant. In Stalingrad many years ago men died on the shore holding rifles and ammunition. The Russian Army didn't have enough rifles to fight the war. They would pair up, two men at a time. One with the rifle, the other with a magazine. When the one with the rifle would die, the other would pick up the rifle and proceed.

A PLACE TO BURY HORSES

Marybeth opens the door to Bones, who looks, more than anything, tired. I realize the stress I've put him through, and I am ashamed. He holds within his vice like grip a white paper bag, from a pharmacy. I look to him, my face swollen and broken, and he sighs under his breath, before walking over to me. He gives the bag to Marybeth, who at this point has placed the rifle back by the door. She walks past me quickly, wordlessly, and goes to the kitchen. Bones follows her, and closes the door behind her. When he turns, I see a friendship partly die upon his face. He shakes his head, and comes over to me. He sits at the edge of the couch, as I listlessly stare at the ceiling. I look at him, studying. I don't know what he's thinking, as he wipes his face with his hand, runs a hand over his head. He turns, after a moment.

'What the fuck have you done?'

I turn away, closing my eye.

'Joel, what the fuck have you done?'

'Christy –'

He sighs, angrily.

'Joel, what did you *do?*'

'I...Christy. Okay. Something bad happened to her. Involving work. The fuckers who did this to me.' It's an admission I hadn't allowed myself to say. They were involved. It's almost as if the beating validated it. Confirmed it. I'm waking up.

A PLACE TO BURY HORSES

We talk for a while, but the concussion is too much.

I sleep the rest of the night, nightmares scarring the dark. I see Christy as a corpse in the woods, her face skeletal, beckoning me into a foreboding mist that stretches through forever.

I wake up, purposeful. No more could be said. Nothing more to do – save for go for a drive with Bones.

*

OUTSIDE OF ROME, OREGON
IN THE CAR.

There is a quiet in the golden haze of the afternoon as myself and Bones drive to my apartment. I need to get my 1911, and the bullets. Hell, might take the book on a memory stick, too. No harm in finishing what I've started, in every way. We pull up outside, just down the street. It's all clear.

I haven't told Bones anything yet – no point. Will do later, when I need to. He's already offered for me to stay with him and Marybeth at the ranch. I accept – though I know in some part of my heart I wouldn't be staying too much longer.

'Joel, someone you're looking for?' He asks as I scan the street again. No sign of Vera, or McKinney, or Tony. No one seems to be staking out my apartment – least for now. They might even think I've died. I shake my head, as a woman walks past with a pram.

'No. I'll only be a minute, okay?'

'Sure. Just clothes, right?'

'Right.'

A PLACE TO BURY HORSES

I head out of the car, Bones keeps the engine running. I head to my apartment, the door still showing a bloody handprint. I sigh, as I open it. I head to my room, pack clothes, save the book to a memory stick, throw that in. At the bottom, I place the 1911 and the spare magazines. I also put in a box of .45's. I head back out, and straight out of the front door again.

Feels like I will never be here again.

The sun is a golden orb of fire, but in the distance I see a distant dark cloud, bringing with it the promise of rain. I stare at it for a moment, as I light up a cigarette. My eye burns and aches, and my face still feels as if it is made of shattered glass. But for a quiet moment, I feel something akin to calm. I feel the sun wash over me, and I close my working eye. We drive for a while in silence. The forest is dark and deep. *Cromarty High* plays over the radio. I reach over before the song brings up memories and kill the radio. Bones breathes deeply and sighs.

'Joel, what are we doing?'

'Thinking. We're...I'm, I'm thinking.'

Eventually, we pull into a small diner. I think we're near enough on the way to Portland. Don't know what we're doing. It's a building of glass and baby blue wood – a waffle hut. We sit in the parking lot for a time. Bones smokes, I join in. Everything feels as brittle as shattered glass.

Bones looks up at the sign. *Maggie's,* the neon states. The air is cool, but there is warmth hidden within.

'So...I guess you're staying with us, huh?'

'Bones, I...'

'I'm pulling your leg,' he says with a smile. He breathes smoke out deeply. 'Just presumptuous of ya.'

'Shut up,' I say. I feel a smile at the corner of my mouth. 'I know you love hanging out with me.'

We laugh. We allow ourselves a moment away from the horror. We go inside and eat. I'm half way through a plate of buttermilk chicken and sausage gravy when I see her. Bones is telling me about a relative of his in Queens – he runs a nightclub, and yes, he could do with security. Bones could set me up with an apartment in New York. He has friends, he says. The kind that he trusts enough to help. I wonder what that is like.

He pauses when his phone rings, and he fishes it out of his pocket. He coughs once into his closed fist, and smiles.

'Just Marybeth. Can I take this?'

'Sure. Of course.'

Bones smiles and stands. He walks over to a jukebox, above which is hung a painting of the sea. I look out to the car, and see Christy sat cross legged on the hood. She's wearing the clothes she wore when we held hands on the pier. I know she's not real. I know it. I don't know what is happening to me, anymore.

The ghost outside tucks her hair behind her ear. She looks over to the forest, and smiles. Her hands are covered in roses. She turns then to the window, and sees me. Smiles. She blows me a kiss, her smile warm and delicate, and I feel my good eye tearing up. I close it, and when I open it she's gone again. Like the smell of summer getting lost in the beginnings of the autumn breeze. Bones comes back, I hear him sink into the seat.

'Sorry about that...Joel? Hey, you okay?'

I turn to him with a bloodshot, tear stained eye. My face hurts like someone had beaten me with a mallet.

'I...' I run a hand over my face, wipe away tears. 'I don't know.'

*

BONES'S HOUSE.

AFTERNOON. UNSURE OF TIME.

We don't speak on the drive home. Bones, unquestionably, was worried. He casts cursory glances to me, the forest. The night draws in, and the gold of the day bleeds away. Like a bleeding brain, or a child as they die in the night and the rain, swaddled in the wreckage of a car.

We get out of the car, and Bones watches me quietly. He doesn't say anything. I sit outside. I'm tired of ghosts. I wonder if Bones or Marybeth could see them in me. Those things behind my eyes. I sit on the chair on his porch, and just stare out at everything. The world, maybe.

After a while, Bones comes outside. Inside, I heard arguing. I think I am bringing out the worst in them. I understand.

He steps out into the dying day and slams the door. He pinches the bridge of his nose, and sighs. He looks at the forest, and the horses. The sky is a shade of purple.

He looks at the sky, and not at me. He looks down, clenching his jaw. His eyes are closed.

He places his hands on his hips, and when he looks up, I see his eyes are red.

'Marybeth wants you to go.'

'I understand.'

'I...I don't.'

I nod. Close my working eye. I light a cigarette, and smoke on his porch. He's silent for a minute, then speaks.

'What's the play?'

I shake my head, drop ash on the oaken porch.

'I don't know.'

'I'm not hurting anyone.'

'I know.'

'I'm not letting you hurt anyone, either.'

'Yeah.'

He shakes his head, looks down. Closes his eyes, and nods.

'You know that, right? I can't...I. I have a wife, Joel. I'm with you, but this...you need to, have to stop this.'

'I know.'

'So how can I help?'

I wipe my face, and I forget about the wounds. My face still is broken. I think for a minute, the pain focussing me. I turn to him, tapping more ash to the floor.

'You still know how to pick locks? I need to borrow your car, too.'

*

I sit parked just off the road that leads to the Pearl. I'm losing track of time. Don't know if the moon is rising or falling into the sea.

I hear, gently, Christy breath in the car. I turn to her. She looks ahead at the forest. Doesn't speak, for a while. I smoke.

'What are you doing, big guy?' she says. I shake my head. My skull burns, and I lower my head.

'I don't know.'

'You do,' she says, 'because I know you do.'

'I know.'

Me and my ghost. We are forever here. I think for a second, just for half of one at a push, about Alice. I don't know why she appears, why she's there in the back seat. She's there for a moment. Touches my neck, gently, and kisses my cheek. I look in the rear-view and she's gone.

'You never told me that,' Christy says. I shake my head, and turn to her. She's sat facing me, her head resting on the seat. She smiles, weakly, and gently.

'Told you what?'

'The thing you said to her. Before Wyatt. When you left for Crooks Hollow, when you drove away in the rain long ago. That thing.'

'It never came up.'

'But you always think about it. A little. Big guy, it's me. I'm not really here. Part of you. Thing you need.'

'I know.'

'You should speak to her.'

'I know.'

'Joel,' she says, and places a ghostly, intangible hand to my cheek. Don't feel it. 'You have to tell her, before the end. Or at least try.'

'I know,' I say, as a car drives past. I look at it for a while, try to see the driver. I think it's Olive, but don't know.

'I guess it is morning,' I say. I laugh. My father used to wonder about the sun coming up. He was worried it never would.

*

A PLACE TO BURY HORSES

It takes a while for Olive to leave. She sets off down the road, tired and haggard with a car to match. She's yawning. I wonder idly why she never offered Christy a lift. For a moment I wonder if she is even real. Whether or not I was chasing a ghost through the forest, trailing her down into a quiet suburb at the outskirts of Rome. She pulls up and sits in her car for a while. I pull up a few houses down, lower my head. She's too tired. Not focussed. Stupid. Was a time in the desert things like that would get you killed.

She gets out of her car after a moment, and I see she's jittery. She has a nice, white picket fence. Small house. Not many entrances. Probably a back door. I take note of the street, Ennis Lane, and drive past. Number 48. I drive back to the range, to the ranch. I stop, though, when I reach a country road. There is an open field to my left, with a singular tree. I pull over, and get out. Breathe.

I think it must be getting close to winter, and I see my breath on the wind. Carried like scents or perfume. I rest my hands on the wooden fence, and see the sun. I look at my hands – wonder when they started looking as old as they did. I clench my fists, watching the skin work.

I wonder if this happened to my father, once. Maybe he wondered the same thing. Wondered where the time had gone, if he'd spent it well, if there were regrets that he had. Maybe he blamed himself, for being too cold one too many times with my mother. Maybe he regretted the army, going off to fight and kill and lose himself in the jungle. I wonder if he regretted not being there at times, when I was a child. So long ago. Like another life. Scents on the breeze.

I look out at the tree, as the sun casts rays of gold through the branches and dying leaves. I smile idly. I reach into my pocket, fish out the broken phone. Screen still worked. Was just cracked. I idly flick off dried blood and with shaking hands call Alice.

The whole time I feel the nerves in my stomach, icy fingers wrapping themselves through me and twisting. I sigh as Alice picks up.

'Joel?'

'Alice.'

'What are you...are you okay?'

She yawns. Woke her up. Stupid.

'I'm fine. I'm sorry I woke you up.'

'You...no. It's okay. You didn't. I...what time is it?'

'Don't know. Early.'

'Hm. What's up? You okay?'

'Why do you ask that whenever I call?'

A pause. The wind picks up and then dies.

'I. I worry. You know. I worry.'

'I...I forgot what I was going to say.'

Pause. I wonder if her new husband is making coffee and breakfast. I wonder if he loves her like I did.

'It's okay. What did you wanna talk about? I'm, you know. I have work in a little bit, but can stay if you need to talk?'

'I...' *Wyatt dies in the car. Rain.* 'I just wanted to say something, you know. A friend, she...she's more than a friend, but she told me to, to talk to you. You know.'

'Oh? You're dating?'

'Not the point.' I catch my own tone. 'Sorry. Yeah. Um, took a lot. But yeah.'

'That's...that's great, Joel. Really. I mean that. Good.'

'I know.' I smile. I think Alice does the same. You can tell when someone speaks, even if you can't see them. I think about Alice's smile and stop.

'I'm sorry,' I say. 'For Wyatt. The thing I said before I left with him. What happened after.'

'Joel...I...I know. It's not your fault. I was...I was hesitant, you know, when...'

A man's voice. Distant and echoed.

'Hon? Who's that?'

'A friend, she's just upset. Sorry.'

I nod. She lied too easy. Don't know when that came about, when she got that skill. Then I realize. Probably because I'm speaking to her.

'Okay,' the man says. Her husband says. 'I've made breakfast. I hope you feel better soon!' he calls to the woman he thinks is on the phone.

'Joel? I'm sorry, but I have to...'

I'm walking away. Can't hear the rest. The phone is on the floor. I feel snow begin to fall. Eventually, the phone will be buried there, cracked and covered in my own blood, till it falls apart.

I will never speak to Alice again.

Never again.

*

ROME, OREGON

EARLY MORNING, BEFORE *THE PEARL* CLOSES.

Bones and I sit in the car, as we drive. Before, when I turn up, he asks where I'd been all night. I ask him if he's told Marybeth that he was going to help. Neither of us answer. Still, in the car, I feel something approaching terror. I don't know, in all honesty, what I'm doing.

'So, we're...what, exactly?' Bones asks.

'We're breaking into someone's house.'

'Why?'

'The police won't,' I say. I look out at the window. It had snowed all night, and now everything was sludge. None of it had settled. Melted overnight. Bones is silent. He shakes his head, and sighs deeply.

'Joel, I –'

'You remember that time we had dinner?'

He looks at me for a second, confused.

'What?'

'When we all had dinner. I brought her. You remember?'

'Uh...yeah. I'm...I don't, uh, I don't follow.'

'I hadn't seen someone so low in a long time,' I say. 'Alice, of course. But not in a long time like Christy. I couldn't think of anything. Couldn't think.'

'I...hey, it's, you know. I'm your friend.'

'I know.'

Bones is silent. I speak, now. Feel like it's the most I've ever said to him sober, or without imagining the scream of the M1 Garand, as of late. A thing built on empire, I had said to myself once.

'I hadn't met anyone like her before. She made sense, Bones. It...It was like there had been hole there. It was gone. It was like her little flaws matched mine. Like we fit together.'

'How long did you know her?'

I scowl out of the window.

'Not long enough.'

He nods, doesn't say anything. I shake my head and check our inventory, laid out in the backseat. A crowbar. Lock pick set. A pair of masks. I pick one up, something that looks like the face paint Brandon Lee wore in *The Crow*. Harlequin, I think it's called. I look at it for a second, before raising it and turning it to Bones. He shifts his gaze to me for a moment, before turning away.

'Halloween party last year. Me and Marybeth went as, like, evil clowns.'

I nod. Throw the mask back in the back. I stare ahead. Bones doesn't know about the 1911 tucked into the holster, clasped close to my spine.

*

We parked a little away from her house. The moon had risen. I saw shadows spread across the forests around us. We walked up, our masks on. There was no sign of anyone around, and I watched the street whilst Bones picked a window at the side of the house. I heard the wind rise and then die – like an admonishment of what we were doing. I smiled under the mask. Bones swore under his breath, the lock pick hook in one hand and something resembling a long paper clip in the other. He was turning the lock on the window with the hook, and feeding in the clip at the same time in small increments. He shook his head once, pausing.

'What's wrong?'

He looks at me, just for a second, before shaking his head.

'Nothing.'

A PLACE TO BURY HORSES

I nod. He goes back to work. My mind wanders to the beautiful things we say to each other. The promise of something greater – we do it all the time, to the people we love. Today, we'll be different. The problems we have, they won't matter. I'm as guilty as anyone for that. I wanted things to be better, to provide warmth. Love. To love someone – and for them to love me back. I shake my head.

Christy. Christy was lying in a hospital, with wounds that she may never recover from.

Like a silhouette, or a shadow. Waiting for the light to burn her away.

I close my working eye, while Bones speaks under his breath.

'Got the fucker. Jesus. I'm rusty at this. Fuck.'

I turn.

'Good. Pry it. We'll go in. Wait.'

He looks at me, doesn't speak for a second or two. He closes his eyes under his mask. I cock my head, standing next to him.

'What?'

'Joel, this is fucked. Super fucked. Wait for what?'

'I just want to talk to her.'

'Scare her.'

'Same results. I need to know.' I put my hand on his shoulder. He doesn't recoil. 'What if it had been Marybeth?'

He looks at me, then away again. He peers into the gloom of the darkened house. He sighs, lowers his face. I shake him gently, hand still on his shoulder. He waves his hand dismissively, before placing it – gloved, of course – onto the wooden pane. He doesn't look at me, as he reaches behind his back to the pry bar, where it was tucked into his belt. Feeds it under the window frame.

'Okay,' is all he says. I nod. Good.

*

Olive's house is horrifically mundane. It's decidedly muted – the wallpaper, decorations. Like there had been joy here, once, but had been painted over, or sold at yard sales, or burned in the back yard on a pyre. Bones closes the window behind us, peers outside for a second. There are no stars, anymore. He looks at me, as I wander around her living room. There is a cabinet, with porcelain figures in. Spanish looking. A mariachi, a dancer. I look and them and smile.

'Looks good out there,' Bones says. 'There are no lights in the houses, and...Joel, what are you doing?'

'Alice used to love things like this,' I say. 'I wonder if Christy does.' I gently tap the glass, smile. 'I think she would.'

Bones looks at me. I feel his stare in my spine. He goes over to the stairs, peers up into the gloom. He places a hand on the banister, before looking at me.

'Weird she doesn't have an alarm,' Bones says. He peers back upstairs, and moves up a couple steps. I speak to him as I look into her kitchen, open plan to the living room.

'She probably doesn't think she needs one,' I say. I look around the kitchen, nothing to note. Not even a plate in the sink. If it wasn't for the fact I knew she lived here, this could be a house up for sale. I peer at the starless night from the kitchen window overlooking the back yard. The moon bathes the world in a cold bone colored glow. I almost smile. Everything seems to make more sense, in those quiet moments. When you're alone. I hear Bones come back down stairs, gently.

'No one here.'

'I gathered.' I look back out of the window. Bones stands next to me. He is agitated, I can tell – already planning escape routes, planning the way home. I'm beyond that, though. I don't think I could ever find anywhere like that. It's like I can't make the world make sense. I'm not strong enough. Can't. Reactionary.

'Joel, you're crying,' he says. I nod.

'I know.'

'Joel,' he says with a heavy sigh. Belying a dark heart. 'What are we doing?'

'I said. We're going to talk to her.'

'And then?'

'I don't know.'

'What are you doing?'

'I don't know.' I say. I shake my head, looking at the moon. 'I don't know.'

He leans back, placing his hands on a counter. He stares at the living room.

'We're just going to talk to her,' I say. 'Christy kept fielding calls from her. Said they argued.'

'And you think this had something to do with what happened?'

'No. I'm not saying that. I'm...yes. Maybe.'

'I need more than a "maybe." This is insane, Joel. We're...you; we've broken into her house.'

'I know. I'm sticking to maybe. If I'm wrong, I'm wrong. But I won't be.' I walk back to the living room, move a chair so it's facing the front door. I sit in it, my back to Bones. He doesn't move, but calls to me from the dark.

'Why won't you be?'

'Can't afford to be wrong,' I say. He sits on the couch, and we don't talk much for an hour or two. I put my head in my hands as a migraine stabs my temple as the moon begins to set. Wouldn't be long.

'Head hurting?'

'Yeah.'

'Marybeth's worried about your eye. Worried about the bones there. Who did that to you? You never said, really.'

'Irish guy.'

'Oh?'

'Not much of a singer. His mother is...something. An artist or something. Can't remember.'

He nods. He yawns loudly, before looking at the sky through the living room window.

'Why do we end up like this, in our lives? Do you think?'

'I don't know,' I say. 'I like to think there's something in charge. Don't know.'

'No, seriously. You got the stuff at Point Truth. That shit's just...you know.'

'I do.'

'There was that storm, too, at Agate. You remember? It was in the news.'

'Yeah.'

'I just...' He starts, but doesn't finish for a while. He stares outside. I follow his gaze, watching the night die. He finishes after a while. 'Nothing makes sense, anymore.'

I nod.

'You know, in the army,' I say, 'there was a guy once. Was a marksman. Forgot his name. Not important. This kid, must've been...Nineteen. Twenty, maybe. Young. He'd killed over two dozen men by the time I'd joined. Asked him how he did it. You know. How he killed people, like that, at such an age.'

Bones turns to me, doesn't say anything. I get lost in a memory.

'He says that sniping is like making the world make sense. Everytime he loaded rounds, lifted the bolt. You know. Up, and back, forward, and down. That. He kinda zoned in on the motion, I suppose. He found he could rely on that, when everything else is going wrong. People try and make sense of everything these days. No one can make sense of anything, though.'

'Your point?'

I sigh, heavy.

'You have to make the world make sense.'

He nods. He thinks something of that. I do, too. Something is born there, between us. Understanding. The night fades away. Olive would be home soon. Needed to be ready. The 1911 is heavier, somehow. Like I feel it more. I don't know. Have to get ready. The night bleeds away to grey.

It's cold and misty when she gets home.

*

Olive leaves a black cab, a gym bag slung over her shoulder. She's paler than normal, but seems less jittery than when I'd tailed her. Maybe something had eased. Maybe it was guilt for something lessening. Maybe she just felt better overall. I don't know.

Bones is up and at the door when he hears the cab pull up. The plan is she comes in, doesn't see me in the dark, Bones closes the door. The morality of what we are doing is not lost on me. Can't speak for Bones.

He looks out of the window, carefully, as rain begins to fall outside. I think I remember saying something, once before to myself. It feels like it would rain forever.

He looks over to me, and nods. I close my eye, and sigh. Breathe slowly. Count the breaths and the heartbeats. Calm. Calm is what we need. I look over to Bones, who is stood with his back to the wall next to the front door. There was no room for error, or she'd bolt back outside. I have a feeling she wouldn't call the cops, but the opportunity to get to the bottom of something would be lost. I breathe.

Bones nods once more, as a key is fit into the front door.

*

It's over before it starts. Like slow motion. The door opens, hiding Bones he's so close to it. Olive is putting her keys back into her bag, not looking. I stand, silently, in the dying shadows of the morning. Bones, almost expertly, closes the door. She turns to him, almost not recognising that he was there. He stands, blocking the door. She drops her bag.

'Oh, oh God,' she says. Tries to go for the stairs. Doesn't make it, before Bones takes her arm, and pushes her into the living room proper. She sees me, and the fear is there. I saw fear like that once before, on *a child's face in an upside down car, as his life bled from him,* and *he saw the things that lived in him, and all at once, he was not a child anymore.* I instinctively reach behind me, get the pistol. Sorry, Bones. I see alarm, but he doesn't say anything. Neither does she. The 1911 is heavy. I point it at her center mass and gesture towards the sofa. She's crying. Doesn't go for her bag, where her phone must be.

Like that, it's over. A sense of order is given to things. I sigh, and sit back down. Bones doesn't move from the door. I see the trust in me die though, as he regards the gun he had given me illegally, now pointed at an unarmed woman in her own home. She looks at him, then me.

'Who, who are you?'

'Christy,' I say. 'What happened?'

'I...who?'

I thumb back the hammer, and I see Bones step away from the door. Had to be careful. Didn't want to push him, not to a place where he might let her go.

'Oh...oh fuck, I, I, oh god.'

'Do I need to count?'

'I...oh fuck. It was an accident. We, she wasn't supposed to...we weren't supposed to be caught. We, oh god.'

'Caught?'

'She...' Olive looks at me, crying. She's shaking. 'We...are you the French, or, or the Irish?'

'Do I sound Irish or French?'

'No. But then again I...I don't know. Please don't shoot me.'

'I won't. What happened?'

'Don't shoot me. Please. I don't want to die.'

'I won't. I won't ask again. What happened? Who are the French and the Irish?'

'I...who are you?'

'Concerned citizens.'

'I...oh god.'

'I don't need to kill you. I don't. I could cripple you. This range, I shoot you in the knee, you might lose the leg. Talk.'

'We...my boss, Anthony. He...after, the, oh god...the stuff at Point Truth. The Canadian Mob had lost a lot of real estate in Oregon. You know. The whole...drugs.'

'I don't care,' I say. I lean forward, place the barrel of the 1911 on her knee. I put my other hand on her shoulder. 'I don't care at all.'

Bones takes a step from the door, and gets closer. I look at Olive's eyes, and lower my voice.

'I can't miss, now. Talk.'

'Christy, we...she was my friend. Oh god. She was my best friend.' Olive cries, puts her head in her hands. She shakes and shivers. 'She was my friend.'

'Is,' I say. 'Help her. Talk.'

'We...Christy wanted to run away with her new guy. To Texas. I met him like, twice, both times, I...I was so drunk. Oh god. I wonder how he is. Oh god.'

Bite back. Don't show anything.

'So what did you do?'

'I wanted to quit, you know, stripping. I'm tired. You know. I want to go to New York, and just...lose myself there. I, I...we stole from him. Anthony. Had to.'

'What did you steal?'

'Five bricks of White Claudia. We were going to...I know people, you know, so does she. That would've...she...we needed to find a way out. She said, Christy said, that... if you know something is worth it, you find ways to leave the old things that aren't behind.'

I shake my head. Heard those words before. Marybeth had said them. Christy's damn heart.

I sigh and look at Olive. She's still shaking.

'What happened then?'

'We got caught. Someone saw me acting nervous, put two and two together. I panicked. There's...there's a deal, tonight, ah, oh god. The Canadians and the Irish. They needed the...the Claudia.'

'What?'

'I panicked...I said, I...oh god. I said that Christy was stealing, and, and maybe she'd stolen the stuff...oh, no. We'd split it. The stuff. She took half, I did... I thought that, that maybe she'd get scared, leave town, but...'

It was then I knew that many people would die soon.

'You threw her to the wolves.'

'No, I – '

'This is their land. There are always wolves baying at the door.'

'Please. Please don't kill me. I – don't shoot me. Please.'

'You did this,' I say. I take the gun from her knee, press it to her temple. Lose myself. I take first pressure. Don't even register her anymore. 'You.'

Bones comes over, places his hand gently on the gun. Lowers it. He talks into my ear, quietly.

'That's enough. We're going. It's done.'

I snap back. I'm holding Olive by the nape of her neck tight, the gun pressed to the side of her head. Her sobs are choked out things – cried too much. Recognized the noise from Alice after Wyatt died. Bones whispers in my ear, knelt next to me.

'We're going. Let's go. That's enough.'

I nod. We stand up, Olive sobbing on the couch still. I see bruises already on her neck. Bones opens the door, and looks around the street. No one there at that time of morning. I turn to Olive.

'You know, she thought the world of you. She told me, all the time. You were her friend. I wouldn't go to work for a while. Till this is done, now.'

Olive looks up from the sofa, sickly pale and shivering. She can barely say the word.

'Joel?'

'You didn't deserve her love,' I say as I close the door gently.

Bones and I walk quickly to the car, and drive fast.

*

NEAR PINE OAKS

THE SUN IS BEGINNING TO DIE.

Bones doesn't speak to me. There's tension in the air. I shake. Bones pulls over, nearly swerving. He clenches the steering wheel tight. Doesn't look at me.

'If you weren't already beaten half to death, I'd fuck you up,' he says. I nod.

'I know.'

'What the fuck was that?'

'Talking.'

He punches the steering wheel three times, one time hitting the horn.

'You were going to fucking kill her, Joel!'

I don't say anything. Neither does Bones. He turns the key, starts the engine. Before we drive, he talks, drained. Someone else I'd let down. Someone else. He can join the rest.

'I need you to go, Joel. I can't...I can't let you stay.'

I nod.

'I know.'

'I'll let you get your stuff together.'

'No need. I'll just take a few things...you can throw away the rest.'

I think he hesitates there, but his logic overrules his heart.

'Okay. Okay.'

We drive again. Rain falls slowly. I see a storm tonight. I wonder.

*

The goodbye is sudden, and abrupt, as they all should be. Marybeth doesn't say anything, as Bones has hidden the things we took with us at the range. She wipes tears from her eyes, as I pull on a denim jacket, t-shirt. I leave everything else clothes wise. Won't need it.

I take the pistol, and a couple spare magazines. The box of .45's.

I walk downstairs, and smoke on the porch, a last one. Bones joins me whilst the sky is cracked with thunder and the earth shakes. A thousand miles away, the world is burning raw, or so it feels. We're just getting the feedback.

'Joel,' Bones starts. Doesn't finish for a while. He sighs, lowers his gaze. I turn to him; place a hand on his shoulder.

'It's okay.'

'No, Joel. It's not.'

'I know. It's not. But it will be,' I say. I look to the forest. Such dark wonders lay within I wonder about the devil.

'There's a story,' I say, 'that I heard from a woman. It was about not selling your soul for things that don't matter, I think.'

Bones doesn't say anything, but nods.

'I think there's something to that,' I say. I crunch the cigarette under my boot. 'Maybe it applies to everything,' I finish. I walk. Nowhere to go.

Only through the dark, and the rain. Distant fires upon shores leagues away.

I feel like everything's ending.

*

I walk through the town. I think for a time. I sit under a fire escape whilst the sun dies. It would be tonight, I suppose. Had to be.

Could I?

The thoughts come.

I sit with my back against a wall, and smoke. Bring my knees up to my chest. Think. My ghosts will never leave me. Part of my heart.

'Hey, big guy,' Christy says next to me. I turn. Her hand touches my face, but I can't feel it. 'Cold?'

'It's gonna rain,' I say to no one. The alley is empty save me. 'So yeah.'

'Well that's no good,' she says. Her smile kills anything left in me I could give. I reach out and touch empty air as I gently stroke her face and smooth over her hair.

'You know,' I say, 'you should've just...just, just told me.'

'I know, big guy. I know.'

'We could've just gone to Texas.'

'Yeehaw.'

I smile. Close my eyes. I look at her and see something I could never have again.

'I love you,' I say. The ghost smiles, tucks hair behind her ear. She blushes, and kisses me on the cheek with her ghostly lips.

'I love you too.'

'You know what I'm thinking, right?'

'Yes.'

'What do you think?'

'I think you're going to do it anyway. I don't want you to, though. To feed the earth. I don't want you to.'

'I know.' I sigh, close my eyes again. 'I know.'

I turn back and she is gone. Her ghost dying as the night draws in. I look up, and see no stars. Only clouds. I knew then. I knew what I had to do. I was tired.

Tired of the night. The war. It all. Had to be this way. Had to be.

Alice, I promise. It had to be. Has to.

*

I call Bones from a payphone. I say I want to give the pistol back, the heirloom of a war and life gone by. I feel the rain gently begin to fall as I enter the booth and punch in his number. Knew it by heart. Not many numbers I call.

'Hello, Bob Rueman speaking?'

'Hey, Bones.'

'Joel?'

'Yeah.' I look around the street, as lights begin to turn on, signs flipped over. I see neon in the windows, and the glow reflects off the wet tarmac and the hoods of the cars, both parked and passing. I look at the forest I can see. Dark shadows, looming over all like something older than time.

'Joel, what's wrong?'

'I was...could I return the 1911? I know it's a little...I just need the money back. That's all. That cool?'

I hear a pause that is filled with the slow gain-filled tide of static. He speaks to Marybeth in hushed tones over the line. Can't make out what they say.

'I...I'm having food, man. When?'

'It'll be a while anyway. Gonna see Christy, you know.'

Pause.

'Yeah,' he says. 'Okay. Have you got somewhere to stay?'

'Yeah,' I lie. 'Gonna get a motel with some of the money. Maybe look at, you know. Moving back to the apartment.'

'You sure?'

'Yeah. In over my head. If it is about what Olive said, the cops'll find out. You know.'

I can't see him, but know he's nodding. I think a piece of him is relieved. I smile and close my eyes.

'I...okay, Joel. No worries. I...what time is it?'

I look at my watch, but he answers himself.

'So it's...7. So, let's say like...9:30? Can you get to Styx for then?'

'Sure,' I say. Check my watch. More than enough time. Could get the rest prepared.

I have the time.

'I'll see you in a while, okay?'

'Yeah,' I say. He hangs up. I stand there, the phone shaking in my hand. I wipe something wet from the corner of my eyes. I sigh, and think. It takes me a few moments to muster enough of myself to leave. I catch a bus to the hospital. Time for goodbyes.

Rain.

*

There is a shadow over the ocean and moon when I arrive. I walk past reception, smile and wave. They know me by now. The elevators reflect and distort, like they always do. I stare into my face. Beaten, swollen. I still don't know if there is damage done to me.

Stupid. Should've killed them all in the car. Stupid.

I grit my teeth. Close my eyes. I punch the wall. Stupid.

I get off on Christy's floor, and walk to her room. The lights of the town bleed through the window like stars. She still lies in bed. I smile, frown; and then open the door. I gently close it behind me, *the click akin to the bolt of the M1*. It echoes in my head. I smile then shake my head.

I take a seat next to Christy, and gently hold her hand. A few drops of rain begin to fall on the window.

'So,' I say. 'This is...It's probably the last time I visit.' I close my eyes and lower my head. When I open my eyes I'm staring at the floor.

'I never...there was something I should've said.' I raise my head. 'And something I shouldn't have. A long time ago. Before you. To someone else.'

The thing I said.

'I was married, you know. Alice. She was...she was my childhood sweetheart.' I shake my head. Smile.

'Something changed when I got back. I took an AK round whilst behind a wall. Didn't get it for, you know. Saving someone, or. Doing something.'

She doesn't move. I squeeze her hand.

'Alice, she...she tried. I was drinking alot. Some was I.' I feel my eye get sore, and teary. 'I don't know why. Not at first. Felt like...Like it was something that always was.'

Nothing. *Rain.*

'Alice tried. You know. She did. Everything was different. I never knew my son. Didn't know myself. Saw a woman die in my arms, calling for her child. A man with his face blown off. A pregnant woman shot to pieces in the back of a car. Things. I can't.'

Don't realize I'm crying. Don't get why. Always on my mind. Reminders, burned into a nightmare that plays out every time I close my eyes.

'The truth is, though. I. I miss the war. I do. Something about it. Routine, maybe. Something that made sense. I could never feel at home after I came back. Was like I was always home over there.'

I look at Christy. The beep of the vital monitor is louder in silence. I'm lost in a memory of *Alice, sat on the couch I wasn't there to help her pick. I'm sat on the recliner, waiting for Wyatt. We're going to a funfair for Halloween, at Crooks Hollow. A circus. I hear Wyatt singing in his room whilst he gets his costume on. Alice doesn't want to go.*

She smiles at me, and I smile back, before it wavers. The thought I've had since I was home bleeds to the front of my mind. I look at her blankly.

'Joel? You okay?'

Had she been speaking to me? I don't know.

'I'm fine. I'm. Yep.'

'If you don't wanna take him, that's, you know. It's a lot. Been a rough few months,' she says. I nod.

'Alice,' I say. She smiles at me warmly.

'Yeah?'

'I love you.'

'I love you to.'

I lower my gaze to the floor.

'I want a divorce,' I say. She laughs quickly. Thinks I'm joking. I carry on.

'Already have my things packed. Upstairs. We'll talk when I've brought Wyatt back. I want a divorce.'

'Okay, you can stop joking. You dick,' she says, smiling. I can see it wavering though. I look at her, my eyes focusing on things past her.

'I'm not. We'll talk when I'm home.'

'Joel...I, wait. What?'

'I'm...I don't know.' She starts to cry. I hear Wyatt come downstairs. I go to the door, whilst Alice cries. Halloween decorations at the window. After that night they are not taken down for months. Wyatt is dressed like a cowboy. Or a skeleton. That part is hazy.

He sees Alice crying.

'Mom?'

I put a hand on his shoulder, crouch down to his level.

'Mom's just a little upset because she just heard some bad news.'

He runs to his mother and hugs her. The last time. She looks at me with red eyes. I'm ashamed. Not guilty. Something more.

'Come on, kiddo,' I say. 'Mom needs some time alone.'

Wyatt nods, and kisses his mother goodbye on the cheek. We go outside to the car, and the last thing I see is Alice looking at me with wide, red eyes.

I'm back in the now. Shaking. I look at Christy, breathing ragged and tears on my face.

'So now, you, you-' I can't finish. I stand up and kiss her gently on the forehead. I take my dog tags off. Forget I wear them. I leave them on her bedside table, as the rain begins to pick up. I kiss her hands, paper thin. I regard the approaching thunder. See it low over the dark and graven clouds. I think for a moment, before regarding Christy.

She is frail, dying. I close my eye, the working one. I kiss her gently on the forehead.

Distant thunder. A sign of things to be.

*

STYX LANE GUN RANGE
LATE, WITH A FULLMOON

I stand outside, under a wooden canopy, looking at the road leading to the range. Haven't seen Bones drive up yet. I have time to think and consider. Could call Farrows. Tell her what Olive said.

I won't, though. I know that. I instead think of the dead.

Is everything better for our passing? They ask, these ghosts.

No, I say. My father and grandfather stand there, in the dark of my mind.

Why did I give the world its greatest victory? I killed the Nazi's on the shore for you to be free, my grandfather says, a Thompson in his hands. My father, with the black plastic of the M16.

And why did I give everything up? For you to squander, and hunt for black gold in the desert, for a country choking itself to death?

I light up a cigarette and stare into the dark of the night sky. Nothing more to say. Bones drives up the road, the only car. His lights are the eyes of some God as they pierce through the rain. I nod at him. He sits in the car for a moment, before he gets out. I smile. He does the same, but his is weaker. Maybe he knows in this moment. Maybe.

'Hey, Joel.'

'Bones.'

He looks up at the starless sky.

'Man, this fucking weather. I got ya money in the office safe, so we'll, you know.'

'I do.'

We walk through the door after he fumbles in the cold for the keys. He coughs a couple times. Fighting something in his lungs.

'You okay?'

'Tired. Don't know if you remember, but I didn't sleep last night.'

I nod. Nothing to say to that. Lower my gaze, head. The rain picks up. He pats me on the shoulder as we walk through the room, guns on the racks. I pass the M1 Garand, whose scream had echoed in some part of me since I took second pressure some time ago. Don't even remember when I shot it. Seems so long ago. I feel as an older man, now, since then.

Bones speaks.

'I'm glad, dude, that, you know.'

'Yeah.'

'You gone to the cops, right? To say that Olive had said something?'

'Yeah. Said she came to me because she was guilty. Not her fault.'

'Yeah. Good.' He drops his hand as he opens the office up. 'Good.'

He walks over to the seat where he once had given me the pistol in the first place. The room seemed smaller somehow. He turns on the light and sits and the desk. I sit opposite.

'So, you're wanting me to take it off you, yeah?'

'Yeah -'

I smile at him, as I draw the gun. Level it at him from across the desk.

' – About that.'

He looks at me warily. Think he can't really believe I've pulled the gun on him. Fuck it. I thumb back the hammer. He raises his hands.

'Joel, what the fuck?'

'I need you to handcuff yourself to the desk, Bones. It's bolted to the floor. You put them in the top drawer of the desk, after we went to Olive's. I saw you. Saw the drawer was empty.'

'Joel,' he starts, but doesn't finish. He opens the drawer, handcuffs himself to the leg of the table. I ask him for the key, and he gives me it. I pocket it, not lowering the pistol.

'I need your phone, too. And the key for the ammo and trigger locks.'

'Joel, what the fuck are you doing?'

I shake my head, a weak smile on my face.

'Dreaming,' I say. I take first pressure on the trigger. He does what I ask. Fishes into his pocket for the keys, and gives me his phone. I throw it over my shoulder, far away from him. The keys, I take. I look at my friend, and regard him. There's fear there, in his eyes. Something cold in his heart. He hated me, maybe, but think it was just that I'd broken his heart.

I pull the trigger, and it clicks empty. Bones doesn't flinch, or turn away. I see surprise for a second, though.

'I wouldn't shoot you. You're my friend.' He talks to me gently.

'Joel, if you...you, you can't. I...they'll, you can't.'

'I can do what I want. Like everyone. The world still turns.'

'Joel, please. Please. Don't. Don't. Let me go. We can, I, please. You...Joel, this, it...'

I close my eyes. Run a hand through my hair. I look at Bones and see the plea in his eyes. The thing his words are failing him, his eyes say. Things like that, and more. None of it feels real.

Head hurts. Eye's still fucked. Need to focus. I once had a child. I think about him. I turn to Bones, and speak gently.

'I'll call the police in an hour. Tell them I heard shots. I'll tell them someone stole guns.'

'Joel –'

'Goodbye, Bones.'

I close the door to Styx Lane, to any semblance of order. Under my arm, I carry a rifle that once had been used to fight on Normandy, in Guadalcanal. On the keychain for the locks are Bones's car keys. I close my eyes, and think of Christy. Everything ends, eventually.

*

PINE OAKS, OREGON

NEAR THE END.

I step out into the rain, and feel it beat gently on my head.
I hold the Garand by my side, the pistol in the holster on my hip. I
step out into the night. I walk a slight time, just across the gravel to
Bones's Chevy. I slip the rifle onto the passenger seat, and stare at it.
There's water in my eyes. Can't see out of one eye still. It's fine. It'll
all be fine. Won't need it much longer.

I drive a short time, straight to *The Pearl Palace*. Christy
used to dance here. She'd never dance again. I don't forget that, not
for a moment – I say it in my mind as a mantra. I wondered once if
damage, in some dark, deep well of me, my mind, has been done. I
think maybe it had. Don't know. The signs bleed neon into the dark,
red and pink lighthouses to guide me there. I see a man stood outside
in a suit, smoking. A few women wear long dark coats to hide
themselves, their skin. I get it. It just doesn't mean anything
anymore. Won't mean anything. I look at my face, my cheek stitched
and my eye swollen, in the rear view mirror. I wait for them all to
go back in, and then take the rifle.

They'll blame the war, of course. I know it already. The
trauma, of losing Wyatt. Make my son a martyr. Something to
explain away what I'm going to do. Not for me. There's no recourse.

A PLACE TO BURY HORSES

It is simply that long, long ago, rules were set, and they don't change.

I pull back the bolt on the Garand, and take one of the boxes of 30-06 and load 8 of them into the last unloaded black En-Bloc clip. Long brass angels. Every bullet has a bed made for it. I put the clip carefully in, and the bolt springs forward, closing the chamber. Lifted rounds.

The click is loud in the silence of the car, but already I can hear the music. I recognize the beat – a methamphetamine pulse. I imagine *Christy on the pier, telling me about her horses*. She wanted to ride horses for a living, go back and start her life again. Now her spine was leaking fluid, and her face was gone, and a dozen men and women – all of them smarter than me – are still trying to make her whole again.

I see the bouncer, now, step out of the purple neon of the doorway. He's a big guy. His name...it's something Irish. I remember him giving me the thumbs up so very, very long ago – as I watched Christy disappear into rain. I stare at him through sheets of water that lashed at the window. He's smoking a cigarette, looking up at the moon with a smile. His hand bandaged, from a recent beating. Idly, I wonder if it was mine. I sigh once, before opening the car door. I step onto the mud covered road, a thousand pin pricks of light – a thousand moth bitten holes – in the sky above. I step forward till the red and pink of the sign for the place illuminates me just enough. As I get near I hear the Irish man singing, a soft tone that doesn't match up with his frame.

'As we gather in the chapel here in old Kilmainham Gaol, I think about these past few days, oh, will they say we've failed? From our school days, they have told us we must yearn for liberty. Yet, all I want in this dark place is to have yeh here with me.' He hums a little, and then sees me. He squints in the rain, raising a hand up to his brow to block it. Good. He can't see me. It's too dark.

'Are yeh lost boy?'

'No,' I say. He starts to move to get a better look at me. I raise the M1; punch a near 8mm hole in his chest.

Gunshots don't work like they do in the movies. There's little in terms of the wide spread of kinetic energy – he won't go flying back, or anything like that. Only way that could happen is if the bullet was that high a calibre it'd throw me back too. It's a singular point of impact – the kill comes from shock and blood loss, as the bullet twists and spins inside him; not the actual initial bullet impact.

That won't do. I need him down. If I wait for the shock and blood loss, he'll choke the life out of me; beat me to death in the rain and the mud. Still remember the alley. Won't do at all.

Another gunshot follows. He's a big guy, doesn't go down still. Needs more. He lurches out of the light into the dark, and I hear his chest making a weird sucking noise; like a sewage filled pipe, clogged. His heart was beating fast, and his life was spilling into the mud. He takes a swing at me, almost drunkenly. I duck under it, loose my footing.

Stupid. I fall on my ass, into the mud. He kicks me hard in the ribs, and feel one break. I grit my teeth hard against the pain, whilst he's trying to damage into me with his boot. I fire another round, this one hitting him a little under his left eye. I feel warmth on my face; and I realize there are pieces of him all over the ground, on me. I look through his blood at his body, as it shakes and shivers in the rain. His eye fills with red, and I see meat coming out of his head and mixing into the deluge. I drink the night in deeply, the pain in my side making me want to be sick. Christy won't dance again. She's too busy dying in a hospital room in a coma.

I stand up, my rib creaking under my weight. Fired three rounds, five left before I have to reload again. Make them count. I step forward, holding the rifle by my side again. I step over McKinney's body. McKinney, that was it. That was his name. His mother was a painter.

I go to the doorway, seeing the familiar purple and red neon, painting everything in a Vaseline haze. Music blares, loud. Can't think straight, too loud. Focus. Don't think about the guy who you just killed, or the many more you have yet to. Think of Christy, the other girls who could end up like her. Think about them.

A PLACE TO BURY HORSES

I step past the reception; the guy in the suit has his back to me, looking at some coats that guests must have left. He turns around, sees me. He starts to say something, but I level the Garand at him. He goes quiet. Sits down in the black leather chair behind the counter. I nod, and he raises his hands. Good. I take a step forward; hit him with the butt of the rifle. He goes limp, and I see teeth hit the floor. It's fine. He deserves a few marks at the least. I step past him, and see rooms off to the side, lining the right hand wall. More music pulses into my head. I smell sweat. I see a young girl wearing something that looked like it was made of belts step out of a room. Her eyes are wide, green like the leaves of a tree in spring. I remember the horses on my Pa's ranch in Texas. When they were scared, how their eyes looked. I shake my head when she opens her mouth to scream, and she closes it tightly. Her bottom lip shakes. I try and remember her name, but can't at first. Saskia, that was it. *"The new girl,"* Antony had said to me, once. *"Straight offa boat."*

I motion with the rifle to go back into the room, and she does. I take a moment to focus on the rainfall that I can still hear from outside. The pitch-black night hid it, but I knew, deep down in some valley of my heart, that I was right, so long ago – it'd rain forever.

I step past them, and see stairs going up to the main bar and club floor. I take a minute to catch my breath, breath some of the blood from my lungs. Rib hurts, head hurts, still can't see. Keep pushing. Get through it. Been through worse. I remember the desert.

A PLACE TO BURY HORSES

I see Sara, who offered to love me once, sat in a circular
booth with some kid who looks nineteen. He's shaking a little. His
face is slick with sweat, but Sara is trying. More girls and people are
filling the floor – the girls wearing things that'd take the innocence
of anyone who went in there. I'm not looking at the girls, though. I
keep it simple. I try and pick out the potential threats, looking around
the club. The music and the rain must've hid me. The night no doubt
had a part. I stand, walk up the staircase, and level the Garand at the
nearest man who could've been a threat. The lightings making it
difficult – it's too fierce, loud. I scan him, looking. See a pistol,
tucked into the waistband of his trousers. Canadians and Irish, Olive
had said. I manage to line the guy up with the front and back sights,
before anyone sees me crouched in the dark of the staircase. I
squeeze the trigger, and see him drop with a hole where his eye and
a large portion of his face used to be. Shorn like sherbet – he dies
before he meets the ground.

The screams start, and I stand up now. One of the wise guys
shouts in French at me, pulling out a little revolver, black and matte.
I shoot him in the collar bone, then place another in his chest. I see
blood hit the wall behind him. As he slides down it to where he'd
stay till later when the cops came, when he'd be grey and cold, I see
a bullet hole. A rose dug into the wall, made of his life blood and
steel. I fire another shot at another guy I see stand up by the bar, but
it's wide. Sara is running past me, and then the others join. Can't
move. Crushed. I hear the *ping* of the clip as it flies out, cold black

steel on the linoleum floor. I see more guys coming from the back rooms with guns, silver pistols and revolvers glinting at me dangerously. Gotta move. Get out of the crowd, get cover. *Move.*

'Kill that wanker!' roars an Irish man, wearing a blue suit and with dark curly hair. I struggle to force my way through the crowd, and I'm feeding the clip into the open chamber on the Garand when the first round whizzes by my head. I hear a noise behind me; someone took the hit. I can't look. Won't. Gotta move. I snap the clip in, taking a knee just in front of the staircase. The crowd moves around me, stones in a river. I'm conscious of the people. I'm worried about a couple things; mainly that the things that miss me could end up going through them. My bullets, too. 30-06 in this kind of place would be like shrapnel from a hand grenade with ricochets.

I'm thankful when I see the crowd finally push around me, and I fire four rounds at a guy by the back room doors. Gotta find the office. *Think, Joel, think. Where was it?*

A gunshot shatters the now empty air around me, splintering the wall to my left. I fire another round, and this time the guy in the suit goes down. He's clutching his throat, so I fire more rounds at him till the clip comes out. I lost track of another couple guys because of the crowd. Not good. Keep alert, try and focus through the music. Focus.

I see one of the wise guys screaming French at me, his eyes wide and wild. He appears from behind an overturned table. He shoots at me with the pistol in his hands. By the time I return fire and he falls silent, I feel a punch in my collarbone, just off center of my chest, and a searing hot scratch on my temple. It's like someone whipped me with fire.

Real problem is I have blood in my eyes, now. Not good.

Can't see.

I hear more shots from the bar and I drop a knee, putting a clip in and firing blind. I hear someone yell, see a red stain on the mirrored background behind where his head was. Good.

The bolt snaps back, and when the clip flies out and hits the floor with the cold metallic clink I'm thankful. One clip left, and I think only one guy, then Antony. I step forward a few times. I'm in the middle of the dance floor when I hear gunshots, and feel a sharp powerful punch in my shoulder blade. I hear another shot go past, and I try and turn and raise the Garand, but my left arm isn't working anymore. The Garand clatters to the floor. The gunshot must've done something and I drop quickly, fall to my back. I pull the pistol out, the 1911. Click the safety off and thumb back the hammer, and feel a bullet hit my hip. Stupid. Didn't look around, wasn't careful. Stupid.

It was Vera, that older woman with the 1950's doo wop vibe. She has mascara running down her face, and anger in her eyes. I shoot at her with the pistol, five or six violent heartbeats in the pulsing music of the club. She drops to her knees first, and then onto her side. I stare up at the ceiling; close my still working eye for a moment. I stand after. Hip felt like someone had drilled into it, left arm still numb. I stagger to my feet, but I need to kneel for a minute, catch my breath. I didn't know where Antony was. Wasn't one of the guys I shot. I step over to Vera. She's twitching, and holding a place on her chest just to the left of her heart. Blood's coming out between her fingers, and I see another two holes on her, one near her stomach, the other above a rib – the white shirt she wore staining red like a napkin lapping spilled wine. She looks up at me with her eyes still angry, blood dripping from her mouth to the floor. She was drowning, and did it while still hating me. She started to speak in that Brooklyn accent again, her voice thick and clogged with blood. Life was leaving her in a crimson wave.

'Why are ya doin' this? We never hurt no one who didn't have it comin, ya fuckin, ya...'

I interrupt her with a .45 through her temple. I see the things in her head hit the floor and spread out in the red puddle that was forming.

'Because I'm tired,' I say, standing. I drop my jacket on the floor, so I'm just wearing a black t-shirt. I see red stains all over the denim, and I can't bear to wear it anymore. I step over the Garand, still on the floor. I look at my left hand, and see the fingers twitching and shaking. No good. Can't shoot like that; must've been in shock. I feel my legs give out for a second again, and I collapse to them.

A PLACE TO BURY HORSES

My bones feel like glass. The leg I hurt in the war screams at me in lashes of fire. Adrenaline was making me shaky, and I felt blood leaking down my back. My arm felt cold, and my hip was beginning to numb now. It was like someone had put ice to it. Shock setting in, my heart pumping blood out faster and faster onto the ground than I can handle. I force my legs to work, standing up and heading to the backrooms. I stagger to the doorway, and I see the guy with the shotgun come out of one of the V.I.P side rooms, his trousers around his ankles. It's a sawn off, double barrelled.

I manage to throw myself to the side of the door when I hear both barrels fire – cannon fire that ripped through the music of the club, ripped through any silence to be found. I stood quickly, hearing two shells hit the floor in the corridor. I throw myself to just inside the doorway on the opposite side, firing blind. Too much blood in my eyes from the wound on my head. I fire into the guy, punching holes in him till he falls. The slide pulls back, and I drop to a knee. Breathing's not regular. Internally, something irreparable was happening. I'm struggling to stand, now. I rest against the wall for a minute, crouched. I cross my arms, place the pistol on the arch I'd made so I could load it a little easier. I hear the voice of an innocent girl, just turned twenty four, echo in my head. Like static on the radio, I hear her through the pain which was filling me up.

'I thought about what you asked earlier. I, um, I miss my horses', she says, smoking a cigarette. I see something human in the way her lips begin to curl, something loving, and she smiles at me

warmly. She then turns back towards the lake, which led out into the distance to the ocean. 'They're such innocent things. It's, uh, it's dumb, I mean...I'm....you know, what I am. I just kinda wish I'd...I...I wish I still had the farm, you know.'

'What was your favourite horse called?'

She stares out smiling. No answers for a moment, the silence a deep valley in the night, dangerous to fall into. She reaches over with her free hand, the tattooed one of beautiful flowers and her long black nails. Her hand rests on top of mine, and our fingers intertwine. She strokes my hand soothingly with her thumb. I don't see the stripper who lives next door anymore. I see a young girl, someone beautiful, with a whole heart to give yet still. I was wrong, earlier. She still could make it.

'Rose,' she says, not turning. 'My favourite one was called Rose.'

I stand up, back in the now, and I put another clip into the pistol. Standing was the hardest part, now. Staying awake. Everything else is child's play. I'm shivering. Shock's setting in. No. I need to finish this now. Just a little more fire, a little more strength. I don't need to keep it. Just enough, a little more. I don't need it much longer.

As I move along the wall, using it for support, I'm aware I'm leaving a smear that starts at the doorway, and goes all along. I open a curtained off room, and see a stripper crouched, wearing red silk lingerie and nothing much else. She's crying. I step into the room, and take a knee in front of her. She's covered her mouth with her hand, and she's sobbing into it. I think I met her once, whilst I and Christy passed them on the way to the pier, in the rain. Don't remember her name, even if I was told it.

'Antony,' I say. My voice has the texture of broken glass. 'I need Antony. Is he still here? Where is he?'

'He's, oh, God, please, don't kill me. Oh God, Joel, it, it's not my fault, oh God...'

'Where.'

'In, the, the green room.'

'Where's that? I don't remember. I've been shot.'

'End of the hall. Green door, black star. Oh God. Please. Don't. Oh.'

'Go home,' I say, standing. My hip cracks, and fractures from the bullet in it. I could scream, throw up. Feel bile in my stomach. Keep it in. Nearly done. I stagger out of the room, and I see a white suited guy reaching into his jacket in the room across from me. I fire at him, three sharp stabs of the trigger, and stain a mirror at the rear of the room with his insides. He drops something old looking, a revolver. I recognise it as a Webley. He's struggling to breathe, clutching his stomach, and he drops to his knees before I shoot him through the face. He drops, and I set back off down the corridor, and step over Shot-Gun guy. His nose is a bloody hole, and he's leaking all over. I can't look at the wound. It's too much. Focus. Focus.

I see the black star on the green door, and stand in front of it. I close my working eye, knuckling blood out of it. There'd be more of it outside than inside me at this rate. I raise the pistol and shoulder barge the door with my numb left arm. I burst into the office with my gun at the ready; Antony sat there, shells on the oak desk that once – a lifetime, a man, and an innocent girl ago – we had spoken over. He's fumbling with the revolver, and I shoot him in the arm. He looks older, now, seems slower; but so am I. Maybe it was everything catching up to us.

'Yeh mothafucka, yeh sick fuck, ah'll kill yeh, I'll string yeh up...' I try shooting again, but the gun's empty. Clicks. I'd fired too many rounds, not counted my shots. Another stupid mistake. By the time I've dropped the clip and slapped in a new one, drunk from blood loss and my feet swaying, I see Antony has pulled the revolver up. We fire at each other at the same time. I feel a rib go.

Not broken, gone.

The pain is almost unbearable. Almost. I swear I can feel a draft in my body as I pump the trigger of the 1911 three more times. Antony falls to the floor, and I do the same. I feel something on my inside squirm out of my stomach, and I don't look. Guts in my lap. Can't look. Can't. Antony. That's what matters. Him, not me. I crawl along the floor, and I feel more of my life leaving me, leaking to the ground in crimson. Antony is lying on his back, staring at me as I crawl towards him like a snake approaching prey. He spits red phlegm at me, misses. I prop myself up against the wall next to him, and watch him as he looks at me. He manages to get out some words through the holes I put into him.

'Ah'll kill yeh. All this over a stupid hoor.'

'I know.'

'Ah'll say, yeh have no fuckin chance. Yeh dead, boy, yeh fucked, ah'll make sure of it, cunty prick that yeh are... jaysis, yeh fuckin killed me...'

A pause. There are stars in my eyes. I close my eyes and imagine the wind on the pier. Antony speaks quietly, just more than a whisper.

'It almost doesn't hurt. Like it fades. Am I fuckin dyin?'

'Yes.'

'Fuck. Colder than I thought.'

'It's the shock.'

Distantly I hear rain. I'm not sure if it's really here.

'I wanted to die quick,' he says. He coughs, and I see blood on the floor. Seems to be everywhere. 'I want to.'

A PLACE TO BURY HORSES

'I know.'

More of a pause. I look down at my blood covered hands. I would look at the wound, but then the dream would be over.

'I'm sorry about your lass.'

I smile, and think of a girl I knew who had been dying for weeks in a hospital; the lights on, nobody home. She might never dance in the moonlight with her friends, ride a horse named Rose that she left behind in her childhood, in her innocence. I shudder out a breath, and I'm noticing blood leaking out of my mouth in a bloody drool.

'Her name was Christy.'

Anthony looks at me, his face pale. I think I see something akin to acceptance. His breathing is shallow and quick, and I see blood leave his mouth.

'You think that doing this, will change anything? That anything will go back to how it was?'

I think for a moment.

'I can't know that...for sure. Unless I try,' I say.

I fire into him till the gun clicks empty in the silence of the office, the smell of cordite all around me. Antony's face was gone now, jagged bone and red darkness replacing it. I try to stand, but can't. All the weight is on me now. Can't stand, my whole body numb.

Through a window in the office, illumination from the car park bled through. I see the cold dark being replaced by alternating blue and red, the sirens Wagnerian disciples of order. I'm cold. Can think straight, though. Can't move. I black out for a second, a cool wave of darkness.

I open my eyes to the distant shouts of many people, I see Officer Farrows, now, in the doorway. She's got her Glock pointed at me, the black illuminated by the lights outside that tore at the night. Her red hair is dishevelled, and she's sweating. She puts a hand to the black box on her jacket. Swearing into her radio, clipped to near her collar.

'Officer, oh fuck, Officer Farrows, one dead, another critical. In the, uh, the, fuck, the head office.' She raises her hand back to the bottom of the pistol, and points it at me.

'Drop the gun, Joel. Joel, the pistol, oh fuck, drop it. Please. Christ.' She's shouting into the corridor leading back to the bar again, and I hear more footfalls. They're distant, echoing like they were in a cave. The sound of the hooves of a thousand untamed horses, beating upon distant shores, free. I smile, before weakly looking at the pistol, the slide pulled back, empty. My vision's hazy. Darkened vignettes at the edges, coalescing inward in a slowly closing dark circle.

'Officer Farrows,' I say with a slow smile, my throat shards of white heated sand. 'I think I got them all.'

Fading, dying light.

The dark takes over me in a warm wave, and I fall into it with all that I have left.

*

CLOSURE

SOMETIME LATER.

The procession, as Christy heard, was small. It had been a quaint thing, as Bones had said. There were no tears, really, save for Alice. Her new husband and child sat with her at the front, silent. There was a gentle snowfall, the beginnings of winter.

Christy still could not walk, and she had to be wheeled. The therapy would take time. There would be a day when she wouldn't need the chair, though, that was the main thing. As Bones wheeled her gently through the graveyard, they spoke.

'You're seeming better,' Bones says. His beard had become stubble. There was warmth to him, even in the snow. Christy said nothing. Her face was still badly beaten. The doctors had called her a fighter, she remembered. She had been told about what happened in a daze. She knew now what Joel meant when he spoke of dreams.

'I am. Sorta.'

'Takes time, these sorta things... I mean, you're tough, kid. Like, really tough. Can see what...you know, he...he liked, about you. You're like him, a lot.'

'Yeah.'

A slight breeze as they reach Joel's grave. He was buried at Pine Oaks – he never went to Texas. Had no family there. Christy felt she didn't, either.

As they reached the stone, she gently touched the tags that hung heavy around her neck. There was a weight to them that wasn't there before. Something akin to gravity, pulling downward. She sighed and closed her eyes. Bones placed a hand gently on her shoulder.

'It's okay.'

'This is me,' she says. The sun is high, but the sky is white. 'It...I'm so fucking stupid.'

'Hey,' Bones says. He gently squeezes her shoulder, and his tone goes soft. 'You know that's not true.'

'It is,' Christy says. Doesn't raise her head. 'It is.'

Bones shakes his head, and closes his eyes too. He laughs after a moment, a quick thing.

'It's, you know. Joel would've liked the funeral.'

Silence.

'First time he'd have seen Alice in years. She's like you, but, you know. Old. He wouldn't want you to be like this. He did what he did for you.'

A PLACE TO BURY HORSES

'But...I stole the, the –'

'You did what you did because you loved him. He did what he did because he loved you.'

Christy nods her head. The words aren't going in, really. Would take time. They float in the breeze. After a while Christy smokes with shaky hands. Bones lights a cigarette for her, and then himself. They stand underneath a tree. There is nothing to be said, for a time.

***

There is a predawn light, over the snow scarred land. She leads her – knee deep in white – through a winter without end. Low in the eaves of the trees – the soft moan of the disparate wind.

At the edge of the woods, she cusps the dog tags she has held for so long. Round her neck – a momento mori. A reminder that all men die.

Something borrowed, something gained.

She reaches the edge of the forest, with the cold biting to her soul, to the bone. Underneath the low eaves of the trees, where the wind howls and moans akin to a wolf, she stops. The horse shies from the coming wind, over those wicked plains.

'Hey,' she says. 'Hey.'

A PLACE TO BURY HORSES

She touches the flank, taps fingers along the ribs gently. The horse breathes once loudly, then another time quietly. She looks out over the plains. The snow seems to creep into the forever. White ice – created by some higher form of being.

'I just need to do this,' she says, 'and then we can go home. That cool?'

The horse is silent. It looks at the sky, as the dawn creates a razor of light, a dying bead of red over distant mountains. It shakes its head; then stands still and watchful.

She looks towards the trees, the forest, which cascaded into a forever that was lost to all. There would never be a forest as this; never again would nature be as this ever again.

In a low hanging pine, she carves initials. His. The small pocket knife catches the dawn within its blade.

In the snow and dirt and land, she creates a small hole with her hands at the base of a tree. After – when the struggle to stand seemed akin to the fire of some demon, lashing at her bones – she buries the dog tags. Under the snow and dirt, they would last forever.

As she turns from the makeshift memorial, she sees the dawn cast light over a distant mountain. The horse does not shy – it accepts it. Welcomes it.

She runs a hand through raven locks, entwisted.

'I.' She says, but then stops. There are words for this – but they are lost. After a moment, when the wind kicks up the snow, she lowers her head.

'The world wasn't made for you.'

She smiles.

'Or for me. You.'

She lowers her head, shakes it. The snow beings to fall. She regards the horse that Bones had given her. After the funeral. A cold dark night. She touches gently her snout, and the horse regarded the distant plains as though they were born of an older time, and the horse realized it. Something beautiful. Older than time.

'It's okay, girl,' Christy says. She regards the dawn as it cuts lights over the mountain, as if it was born of it and was saluting the land.

'Get you home. Okay?'

She touches the flanks of the horse.

'Rose? It's okay. Everything's okay.'

The sound of the thunder that had hid from the night. Christy looks to the mountains, alongside the horse. She turns, before leading Rose with the lead.

Behind them, the sound of thunder dies. Lost in the wind.

A PLACE TO BURY HORSES

They reach a plain, snow barren. As though the winter was always there, waiting.

'Can I tell you something?' She asks to the horse. Silence.

'I used to have nightmares. For real. Bad ones. Yeah, I know,' she says.

'But I had a dream the other day...feels like I have it all the time.'

The horse walks. After a time, they both stop. Distant highways – a place they both live, now, a vision in the hazy cold distance. An angel from hell and his wife own it.

'I think about when I was young. Things...things make sense, when you're young. Don't they?'

Silence. The wind.

'This...I used to be around horses alot. I knew...we...I used to...'

A pause. She regards the forest that bleeds into the road. Distantly, a gas station. The light blinks and bleeds into the cold air, dismissive.

Christy wipes tears from her eyes. The horse seems to move, to hug her to its flanks. It provides a safety to her. As if she was the same.

A PLACE TO BURY HORSES

'My favourite was called Rose. Like you,' she says. She mounts the horse – difficult, with her wounds. They have healed somewhat, but time is slow and has not provided her enough to be able to mend. They ride off, into that sky lit meridian, down tarmac and concrete. To stability.

Her favourite memory plays in her mind.

A secret told to only him.

Her favourite horse is called Rose.

*

THE END

OTHER BOOKS IN THE AMERICANA MYTHOS

The Visitor

'Some people come into your life to teach you how to let go.'

Point Truth, Oregon.

A grieving woman, who has recently lost her daughter to violence, is greeted one night from a slow-burn shift by a mysterious stranger on her doorstep.

The man offers her a deal: In exchange for complete anonymity, and the promise of 'a call, just once, further down the line', he offers to not only find her daughter's killers but to also dole out some revenge.

When the bodies start piling up, and people she never knew suddenly become capable of the unthinkable, the town starts to implode on itself in secrets, violence, and death.

You don't back out of a deal with him. No siree.

A PLACE TO BURY HORSES

Years of the Worm

Robert Hull, rockstar-alcoholic turned sober horror writer, is greeted one day by an old friend from his childhood; and the next by police, after his friend commits suicide after a grisly crime.

Returning home to North Dakota, Hull has to reunite the group of story-telling friends from his youth, The Nightmare Club, and find out who - or what - has caused so much misery for so many years, and solve the mystery of The Dooley House.

Part haunted house tale, part bildungsroman, and part tender examination of friendship and time, *Years of the Worm* is a horror story about growing up.

Eden Parish

Marlowe has been around a while. He's seen a lot of things, and is always on the run from a past not yet ready to let him go.

When he moves to a cabin outside of Pine Oaks, Oregon, he finds that the past isn't something you can run away from.

A story about responsibility, forgiveness, and also about cruelty, *Eden Parish* is a story where there is no hero, no villain – just the horrible consequences of the past.

It is a celebration of the quiet of a soulless world, one where redemption can be found – but not readily within reach.

A PLACE TO BURY HORSES

About the Author

Connor Grant currently lives in England, with his family and two Chihuahuas, Charlie and Nico.

His first book was *The Visitor*, released in 2016. His second, *Years of the Worm,* continues the Americana Mythos, a series of connected horror tales in a shared universe, all based in Oregon. His third book is *Eden Parish*, a noir mystery/body horror novel set in the fictional Americana Mythos.

When not writing, he tends to be reading, or at least pretending to.

11446866R00180

Printed in Great Britain
by Amazon